Plan B

By DeAnne Hall

"For I know the plans I have for you," declares the Lord, "plans to prosper you and not to harm you, plans to give you hope and a future."
Jeremiah 29:11 NIV

Cover photo by Mistuh Will's phunky photography

Printed in the United States of America

My Purpose Publishing
Charlotte, NC 28213
www.mypurposepublishing.com

Thank You...

Thank you God, the true author of this book, for blessing me with my talent; for Your undying love and favor; for Your Grace, giving me the things I don't deserve and Your Mercy, protecting me from the things that I do.

To the world's Greatest Parents EVER!!! Ira and Pamela Hall I'd give my life for you. You have always encouraged me to do my best. You loved me enough to allow me to experience life with the guarantee that you two would be there for me during good and bad times, trials and successes. You have always been my constant in this inconsistent world. You never gave up on me. I love you more than I'm capable of saying but I try to show you as much as I can. I LOVE YOU!!!

To my other parents Wrenrick and Judy Fetherson, it's hard for some to understand our bond but then again they don't have to because we do. You've been a part of my life since I was 15 and our relationship will last forever. I can never repay you for your many prayers, love and support. Thank you for always being there for me, for loving me solely for who I am. I always know you are just a phone call away. I love you so much!

To my baby, my sister with your spoiled self, Tarsha. I didn't realize at age six that when our parents brought you home that it was going to change my life forever. But it did and I'm glad to say it was a good change. I had my best friend, closest confidant and sometimes greatest foe (LOL) in you. I remember when Nana and Granny Fannie told me that my job, from God, was to take care of you. I did my best and trust me I learned at an early age that God has a sense of humor. You make my life better. You gave me a sense of pride because you were a loving little sister that always wanted to be around me. Although we're older, and you sometimes think you are the oldest. I just want you to know that I'm proud of you, how much I love you and I will always be there for you, just like you have been for me.

To Mister… William Haggins, I'll be the first to say that I never thought and the first to say that I'm glad I was wrong. Thank you for the life lessons that helped me see pass the obvious. Thank you for the love and support, and the laughs. I'm enjoying the journey.

I believe that it takes a village to raise a child, and I had that with my family. (Hall, Cornelius, Houston, Sloan and on and on too many to name them all…LOL) Thank you Ira (Papa) and Fannie Mae (Granny Fannie) Hall and my aunts and uncles you're an extension of my parents. You hold me to certain standards and if you see me going astray you're able to reel me back in. I know that it's for my best interest and it's done out of love. Thank you for the wisdom, prayers, talks and even the discipline. It showed me that you cared and wanted the best for me. You taught me to never give up and that I could do anything I wanted to do in life. My cousins were like my brothers and sisters, and sometimes my partners in crime. Thanks for one of the best childhoods ever and for believing in me even when I didn't believe in myself.

The Fannie Mae Foundation, WOW too many words but I want to say thank you and I love you!!! Thank you for always having my back and supporting me in whatever I did, for loving me in spite of me, for the many meetings at the "roundtable"(we need to get back to that), for the love and blatant honesty and for being there when I felt like no one cared. Love, Always!

To my sister circle; Frenchie, Tiffany, Sennika, Laticia, Annette, Sandra, Courtney, Marge, Krista, Monica, Tamara Bellamy, Tamara Bryant, Eugenia, Nikki, Sylvia, Linda, Luthella, Rosalind, Dianne and Nita I don't know where to start. When I felt weak, you were my strength, you prayed for me. When I was discouraged you encouraged me. When I was sad you cheered me up. When I was doubtful you showed me how. When I felt unloved you gave me your hearts. What more could a person ask for. You have always surrounded me with love and honesty and I thank you for that. I love you ladies and I hope that you know that I'm always here for you!!!

To my loving and protective brothers; Duane, J-Rock, Smity, Ross, Kelley, Thompson, G, Big C, and Showtime Racing MC. Thank you for always being there for me, protecting and looking out for me. Thank you for always respecting me and listening to me when I was trying to understand why life happens and how men think. I lost count of the drawn out phone calls and late night conversations when I just needed to vent and you were there. Thank you and I love you all. (That's the only reason I fuss so much, I just want the best for you!)

To Greater Fellowship Missionary Baptist Church Family, Rev. J.W. Brunson, Sharon and family, thank you for your prayers and positive words of encouragement. Thank you for providing a platform for me to display my talents and always inspiring me to do more. To Mama Armstrong thank you for the many phone calls and words of strength and wisdom and your understanding. I really appreciate it and I love you.

To Dr. Peggy Fuller thank you for being more than my dermatologist, you were my prayer warrior when I had given up on praying for myself. God has a wonderful blessing in store for you, because you are always such a blessing to others.

To Mrs. Patsy Camp thank you for listening and inspiring me. Of course I couldn't have published Plan B without countless Friday meetings as you picked through the words to understand the meaning.

To Mistuh Will, thank you for your artistic eye and the many retakes to please me. I pray that Mistuh Will Photography continues to be an enjoyable blessing for you.

To Tanya Butler and Studio BPA, thank you for one of the best times that I've ever had in front of a camera. Thank you for the many kind words and listening ears. You are such a sweetheart. I never thought that when I met you at Dr. Fuller's event that God was blessing me with another wonderful person to help me to continue to grow.

To Yusef, you already know. Thanks babe and enjoy life!!!

And to all the many people that I have encountered in my life time, if I were to name you all my Thank You page would be a novel in its self. But I want you to know how much each of you has helped to shape the woman that I am today. Thank you so much!!!

Contents

In loving memories...

Mary Cornelius "Mamma" my great-grand mother
Edna Cornelius "Nana"
DeAndrew Cornelius "Daddy D"
Kerry Cornelius
Alfred Morrison
Thomas "Pocket" Connor
Vaudrick Armstrong

You're not with me physically but I carry you daily in my heart. I love and miss each of you dearly!!!

Plan B

Divine remembers how her mind had reeled from Joseph's announcement. What started out as a regular night of pillow talk ended up being a life altering nightmare. Divine laid down as a wife in the 'dynamic duo' that most people deemed the 'perfect couple' only to have her whole world turned upside down.

Her 'wonderful husband' cowardly informed her that he needed some space. Not the 'scoot over, babe, you are on my side of the bed' space. Joseph required the 'I need time to get myself together' kind of space, and secretly some safety distance. He knew that once his latest escapade was discovered it was going to cause great emotional pain for Divine and therefore, possible physical harm to him.

Blindsided and devastated, Divine laid in silence questioning God because this wasn't in her plan. That government issued orange suit crossed her mind more than once. She could have really killed him at that moment.

But this was just the beginning of her fiasco. Seeing him leave was one thing, but not knowing what to do once the door closed behind him was something totally different. She had dedicated her life to this marriage. What else did she know? He was her high school sweetheart- her first love. It worked for her parents. Why hadn't it worked for her?

It took Divine five months just to wrap her mind around the fact that she was single. She had many sleepless nights and lonely days but they kept coming whether she was ready or not. Then came the anger, she couldn't believe that she was going through this. She deserved better. She spent the next eight months trying to get even. But that failed.

Divine made up in her mind that she was going to sue the woman for Alienation of Affection. She felt the woman should pay her $25 every week. Taz, her sister, didn't understand just $25, why not more. Divine explained that she had other children and she wasn't married to her. But just think of the impact, it will be the hardest $25 she will ever spend. Every time that money comes out it will remind her of her part in the dirty deed. As for Joseph, Divine wanted all of his money with the exception of $25. Taz questioned the $25 again. Divine told her that she just wanted him to have enough gas money to go to work to make her alimony. Life would be a struggle and it would be because of the choices that he made. Divine ended up spending hundreds of dollars for three different attorneys to tell her that since they made around the same amount of money, it would be better if she just cut her losses. Be thankful that she didn't have any children involved and move on with her life.

Divine couldn't believe it, even with the proof of infidelity and abandonment they were still telling her that she should just let it go, get over it. But how do you get over it? How do you just get over 14 years of your life? That had been the hardest 18 months of her life until today, when Divine received her divorce papers.

"I hope he's happy" Divine sighs as she signs her divorce papers. She had always given Joseph exactly what he wanted so there was no need to stop now. "I didn't think I would feel this way," she thought to herself as she desperately tried to reach someone - anyone on the phone but to no avail. Not that she didn't have every reason to request the divorce herself, since he had committed adultery, abandoned her in their new home and had a child with the other woman. The child was the ultimate slap in the face since they had been trying for years now to have a child of their own.

Yet here she was at her parent's home in her old room next to her little sister's and across the hall from her parents just like eight years ago. It was as if she had gone back in time or awakened from a long crazy dream.

While sitting on her bed reminiscing she thought of the one that she could turn to, her confidant that she could tell all of her feelings to any time, her journal. How ironic that she opened right to a passage that she had written two weeks after she and Joseph separated.

February 9
It's been two weeks since you've been gone
And as I promised life has gone on.
As I think back I still don't know
What happened to us, and where we went wrong?
I hear sweet songs and a smile covers my face
Then reality hits and tears take its place.
As I think of our past, was it all a big waste?
The devil says yes but that's a mistake.
I've enjoyed my life with my husband my friend,
Surprisingly enough I'd do it again
But different next time in one simple way
The next time I marry I'll let God choose my mate.
Never again will I rely on fate,
Faith is the answer God wants me to wait.
Pray and worship Him, the greatest one of all
And He'll send the man that's worthy of His child.
And with God first in our lives
We will unite as one and be blessed
With His favor until judgment day comes,
Amen

You, me and he...

I have the best of both worlds. I have Joseph who loves to keep me laughing and he makes our time spent together memories in the making. And then there's Lamont my friend, who does no wrong and is a true Godsend. Most women would be pleased to have just one of them but I've been blessed to have them both. I know that I'm going to have to choose one day but for now I have no complaints. I'm here, Joseph is on the other side of the country and Lamont is away at school. My phone bill is the only thing suffering at this point. I spend more on phone bills than I do for my car payment, insurance and gas combined in a month. But I don't mind because that's my lifeline to the men in my life.

I heard the phone ringing from outside. I make a mad dash for the phone nearly knocking my mom over.

"Hello"

"Hey what are you doing?"

That was the beginning of my daily routine. I talk as I walk throughout the house giggling and getting on my family's nerves. "Nothing is that funny" or "anybody on the phone that long must be lying" are common comments spoken as I pass by. Whatever, I'm on the phone with my friend and nothing else matters. We talk hours on end until we fall asleep or the battery dies, whichever comes first.

Taz, my sister, claims she can tell who I'm on the phone with by the expressions on my face. I don't agree with her, but I'm not looking at myself in a mirror either. This particular time I'm talking to Lamont. But if I really think about it, most of the time I'm talking to Lamont, because he's fun to talk to and he really knows and understands me. He doesn't put up with my mess and that's what I like the most. I can have a tantrum and he'll shut me down quick. I needed that strength in Joseph but he didn't have that ability.

Tonight we were discussing children and how we would raise them. I am notorious for hypothetical situations and could get wrapped up for hours on one of my topics. In this particular one I'm pregnant and no longer with the baby's father and wanted to know if Lamont would help me raise the child. Of course he said "yes" - that's the kind of man that he was. How ironic that Joseph beeped in. So I got off the phone with Lamont and continued my hypothetical conversation with him. Now his response was a little different. He required time before he could answer this question but he claimed to love me and was going to form a covenant with me and God. Yet he needed time to answer this and it was only a scenario. It wasn't even reality. Maybe that should have been a sign but I missed it, which is easy to do when you aren't looking for any signs. The conversation went on for a few more minutes and then Joseph had to get off the phone. I love Joseph with all of my heart but I feel like something is missing, I just can't put my finger on it. So, of course, I called Lamont back.

This was becoming a habit. My thoughts, feelings and opinions were lining up with Lamont's more than with Joseph's. But you always hear that opposites attract so I didn't put much thought into it. Besides, Lamont and I were brought up pretty much in the same manner. We both came from the same family structure and were taught mainly the same basic principles and worshiped at the same church. Of course it would be easier for us to be on one accord.

"So what are we going to talk about now?" I asked, as Lamont answered the phone.

"School. Don't you want to finish?" He asked. "Why don't you come here and we can be roommates?" He really thought he was on to something.

"What, now how can we be roommates? What do you think your parents would have to say about that?" I shook my head in amazement.

"My parents know you so that wouldn't be an issue for them.

What about yours?" he quizzed.

"That's a completely different story. Sure my parents know and like you, but you are still a guy. I don't really think my parents would be too kosher with that one." I answered, in shock from his offer.

"Why? It's not like we would share a bed. You would have your own room and I would have mine. The only thing we would share would be the bills and between us that would be nothing." He waited patiently for my response.

"I don't know about that. Besides I was thinking about moving away for a while."

"What's a while?" He asked with a hint of rejection in his voice.

"I'm not sure how long. I've been playing with the idea for a few weeks now. I just hadn't mentioned it to anyone yet." I gave a small sigh of relief after I finished my sentence.

I *thought I was being smart by planting the seed so that we could discuss it later.*

Lamont didn't give in that easily though and continued to probe for answers.

"Where would you go? Who would go with you? What do your parents have to say about that?" He was relentless.

"I know I just told you that I hadn't mentioned it to any one yet, it's still up in the air." I spewed. I *loved being on the giving end of interrogations but hated being questioned about anything.* "I might go overseas to experience something new." I answered.

Finally I had a chance to get it out there. I'll give him a little time to think that over and then I'll let him know that I'm getting married in October. Lamont didn't like my answers and decided to let me know that it was crazy for me to even consider leaving the U.S. so young and alone. Alone, I never said anything about me being alone. That was an assumption on his part, but we were talking way more about this matter than I was ready to deal with so I quickly changed subjects and evidently his heart told him not to object. Not tonight anyway.

"Can you be in love with two people at the same time?" I asked. I wanted his opinion on this one more so to help me understand what I was feeling. I had always felt that you couldn't but if that's true then I really had a problem because I've loved Joseph since I was 15 but now

I care about Lamont almost as much. Of course I started answering the question as soon as I had asked, but then Lamont interrupted me. "You asked me remember." He said and started explaining. "You can care about two people and you can even love two people but you can't be in love with two people at same time. You wouldn't be true to yourself if you tried to convince yourself that you were. You are going to give one that unconditional love that understands, accepts and forgives all. When you are truly in love with someone you care more about their happiness than you do about your own feelings. You go out of your way to ensure that no matter what, you are there for them and it's not about what they do for you or what they have; it's all about what you two possess inside."

Well that was food for thought that I'd have to sleep on. I'd forgiven Joseph for a million things and I accepted him for who he was. I always wanted him to be happy. I knew I was really in love with Joseph. Lamont was such a good friend. He was guiding me towards my heart's desires and had no ulterior motives. That's why I loved him and why he was my friend.

A parent's job is never done...

My parents already knew that I planned to marry Joseph in October, but they were really banking on Joseph going overseas and getting caught up in the single military life abroad and forgetting about me. But Joseph had promised me that we would be together forever and that he wouldn't be happy in Germany until I was there with him. I didn't want to live without him either and I pleaded our case with my parents for weeks until they finally gave in. We were talking in circles and had reached the point where nothing they said was making a difference, so they bitterly accepted defeat and realized that there was nothing they could do to stop us. I know that in the back of their minds they were praying for a miracle but all I could see was being Joseph's wife and having the time of my life through good and bad times because we loved one another.

Bridal books filled the mailbox daily. I wasn't trying to rub it in my parent's faces; I just wanted to have the perfect wedding. We had to have the right location, the dresses needed to be breathtaking and I wanted the reception of a lifetime. I even expected my parents to fund this extravaganza knowing full well they were against it. I understand that since I am their firstborn they wanted to hold on a little longer. But the sight of me in my wedding gown will sway my mom over to my side and together we could persuade my daddy. I already had my sister on my side. I know my mom will change her mind. I must admit she was putting up a good fight. I had taken my sister and my friends to see me in some gowns but my mom was never interested. But this time would be different. I had found the perfect gown and I knew she was going to love it and then she would be ready to take over the wedding plans like all mother of the brides do.

It was time for my nightly phone checks. I called Joseph and gave him an update on the wedding plans, but he seemed distant. I had a wonderful day and really wasn't in detective mode tonight. We chatted briefly and told each other we loved one another and got off the phone. Tonight brought back this feeling that I had while I was visiting Joseph in California back in August. We had hours of eerie silence and I couldn't figure it out. It wasn't just obvious to me either. Our friends noticed it and my girl, Mya, even made the suggestion that we hold off on getting married for a while. Of course, we attributed it to us not being together on a daily basis like we used to and that we would be fine. That was the same vibe I was feeling on the phone tonight. I quickly hit the buttons to happiness and when Lamont answered I immediately heard his smile in his voice. We discussed what was going on this coming weekend. It was Valentine's weekend, and I wasn't really looking forward to it since Joseph was in California. Lamont was talking about some party but I wasn't interested in going and being surrounded by all the couples all hugged up. Not interested, I'd pass this time. Lamont was still going. It didn't seem to bother him that he didn't have a sweetheart for Valentines.

We talked for a little while longer. Lamont had a big exam to study for and I didn't want to keep him up so we cut our conversation short.

"Okay I'll see you this weekend." I said wrapping up our call.

"Actually you'll see me tomorrow. I'm coming home after my exam." I loved it when he surprised me and came home early. We always had a ball when we were together.

"Sweet, I'll see you when I get off then. Good night." I rolled over and placed the phone on my night stand.

Tomorrow seemed so far away. I must admit I was looking forward to seeing Lamont. Plus he's handsome, too. That's always a bonus. I just wanted to go bowling or something instead of going to the party on Saturday but that's just me being selfish. Besides I had plenty of stuff to do in order to get this wedding together. Its hard work doing it by yourself.

By the time I got home, took my shower and threw on some sweats Lamont was at the door. We gave each other a big hug like we hadn't just seen each other on Sunday.

"So what's up for tonight," he asked all enthused.

"I don't care. We could just stay at the house" I replied, his company was sufficient. He grabbed the remote and started flicking. That's how I knew my daddy really liked him; no one, and I do I mean no one, could make themselves at home like Lamont. He was the only guy that wasn't afraid of my daddy either; he looked him straight in the eye and gave him good firm handshakes. He was very respectful and never did anything that my parents would disapprove of, even when they weren't around.

My mom came in the door from work as we were laughing at a rerun of A Different World.

"Do you want to go look at that dress today?" my mom asked, in lieu of hello.

"Hey Mrs. Hill what dress?" Lamont chimed in.

"Oh hey, I didn't see you sitting in there, Lamont. How are you doing sweetie?" my mom said, as she walked towards the kitchen. I know she didn't see him sitting there but she saw his car sitting in the driveway. She just did that to be funny because she knew that Lamont didn't know about the wedding.

"No, not today, maybe next week," I blurted out as I shot a 'please don't do this now' look her way.

"Let me talk to you upstairs for a minute" she said, with a look of disapproval on her face.

The fear of the unknown was invading my mind as I climbed each step. Oh lord, not one of these moments. This could get ugly.

"What?" jumped sharply out of my mouth before I could catch myself.

"Girl don't get slapped. You know you don't talk to me like that." I looked to my daddy for refuge,

"Daddy, Momma just tried to bring up the wedding in front of Lamont."

"I know I heard her. She was wrong with her approach but you are out of order. You're leading him on and you know that man loves you. You don't play with people like that." My daddy had a stern look on his face.

"Man, you two just don't understand..." I folded my arms determined to stand my ground.

"Hush and listen" my parents demanded in unison. They were tag teaming me now. "You've been dancing around this house for months with that 'just a friend' story that only you believe..., maybe? You don't treat people like that. We taught you better than that. You know you reap what you sow. Would you want him to do you like that?" My mom waited on my response.

"No, but it's not like that." I said whining and pouting.

"Well if it's not like that and you two are really just friends, why haven't you told him about the wedding yet?" My parents were showing no mercy. "Go downstairs. Your 'friend' is waiting." My mom was throwing quotations in the air with her fingers as she said friend. I turned and ran for the stairs before they started Round Two. Before I hit the bottom step I heard their bedroom door slam. I slumped down on the sofa and Lamont, obviously concerned, asked if everything was all right. "Yeah, let's go get something to eat." He didn't' ask any questions as I grabbed my purse and headed for the door. I just had to get away for some stress-free air. God why did she do that, I was thinking as we pulled out the driveway. I'm going to have to do some damage control. I just know it.

Even after the turbulence at home we ended up having a ball and neither of us mentioned the dress again that night. I was grateful because I still wasn't ready for that conversation to take place. My parents were right though. I was going to have to tell him sooner or later, but for now I'm going to take the latter of my two choices. When we got back we were full and tired - Laser Quest, one of my favorite pastimes, where you run around a maze shooting laser guns and everyone is a moving target, can really take it out of you. We positioned ourselves on the sofa. He laid on one end and I on the other. I draped my legs over his lap and he cupped my legs with his hands and it was over. We quickly fell asleep. A beautiful end to a much-needed escape.

My mom came and woke us up as she always did and told him to either get up and go home or call his parents and let them know where he was so that they wouldn't worry. He would always go home, but he liked the fact that my mom would offer. "Call and let me know you made it home" she said as she fixed a glass of ginger ale. I climbed the stairs and crawled into bed and waited for the phone to ring so I could drift back to sleep. He made it home safe and sound every time. God always granted him traveling mercies. "I'm here," he slurred

"Okay, good night. I'll talk to you tomorrow" I mumbled. Like clockwork our evenings always ended this way. We were so predictable.

The next day I took my mom to see the dress and it brought tears to her eyes. I knew my mom would love it and I knew that once she saw that I was truly happy she would be happy too.

"You look like a princess in that dress. You are going to be a beautiful bride."

"Thank you, momma I told you that you would love it."

"Are you going to invite Lamont to the wedding?"

"What are you...where did that come from? Of course I am. He's my friend." You could hear the tension in my voice.

"Do you think he wants to come and see you marry someone else?" my mom asked calmly.

"What are you talking about, Lamont knows about Joseph?" I could feel my eye twitching as I answered her questions.

"Do you think a man like Lamont is hanging around because you are such a good friend? Come on baby you're smarter than that. You are only deceiving yourself and it will be you that will lose in the end. Have you prayed about this? Lamont is smart, good looking, treats you like the queen that you are and he loves the Lord. I can really see him being my son-in-law."

Oh my goodness. It hit me like a ton of bricks. Momma was banking on Lamont being the miracle.

"Momma, please stop. I'm marrying Joseph and that's that." I pleaded.

"I know that's what your mouth says but what about your heart? Don't get me wrong, I love Joseph, but a mother knows what her daughter needs and Joseph isn't ready for all of that responsibility. He's just a baby himself and he deserves a chance to grow, live and make mistakes. He deserves to experience life. Besides you two are so young." My mom was still pleading her case.

"There's nothing that we can't do together." I replied. "We love each other."

"If you love each other so much then why don't you wait a few years?" momma was truly frustrated now.

"Watch, Joseph is going to be a good man, just like daddy." I truly believed that.

"Yes, you keep telling me that but your actions say something else. Every time I look up it's you and Lamont and you two are happy. I think you should just finish school and start in your career and then when Joseph comes back, if you two still want to get married then we'll go from there."

"No, Momma, I'm going to marry him and we are going to be just fine."

"Forget it. I can't talk to you. You're not listening anyway. I pray that God can change your mind; you have your mind set on this fairy tale. I'm ready to go. Yes that's a nice gown. How much does it cost?" As if she really cared.

"Forget it. I don't want this one. I'll get dressed so that we can go." I said sadly, feeling defeated as I walked back to my dressing room.

While I was getting dressed my mother was praying to God:

"Father please speak to my child and open her eyes. She's too young to be getting married and moving across the world by herself. I pray that she doesn't make a mistake that she will regret later in life. Please speak to her heart. This I ask in your son Jesus' name. Amen."

The ride home was silent. I didn't want to disrespect my mom not to mention getting an unnecessary smack in the process. Silence is good. It is then that you can hear clearly from God. I couldn't wait to get home to call Lamont; I thought I might hit that party after all. I needed to dance out some frustrations and let off some steam. I didn't even feel like calling Joseph because he'll start talking crazy too. Am I the only one seeing the beauty in this wedding? I called Lamont, but I didn't get an answer. Great, now I really don't have anything to do. I wonder what the Foundation is getting into tonight. *The Foundation consists of my sister, and my first cousins on my daddy's side of the family.*

I couldn't reach a soul on the phone and I mean I tried everybody. This is pretty much how I pictured this weekend anyway - home alone. The telephone ring filled my empty room with life. "Hello," really not expecting it to be for me.

"Hey do you have some clothes on?" Lamont's voice was on the other end.

"Yes," I responded with a partial smile on my face.

"Do you feel like coming out?" he asked.

"I don't care; it doesn't matter" I said lazily, "It's not like I have something else to do."

"Come outside" he replied.

I almost broke my neck getting down those stairs. "Bye, Momma; bye, Daddy," I shouted as I rushed out the door.

"Where are you going?" my mom called out.

"With Lamont" I yelled as the door shut.

We had a ball. We danced for hours, played a few hands of cards and then it was time to go. We had to get back to my side of town before it got too late. We sat outside in front of the house for over an hour talking about the fun we had at the party

"Aren't you glad you went now?" he said with a smile on his face.

"Yeah, you were right for once," I said as I laughed and pushed him on his arm.

"Whatever, you didn't need to sit up in the house waiting on a phone call that may or may not come"

"Shut up! I said you were right. Don't get too grown" I said giggling. "You know you need to respect your elders." I was older than Lamont by five months and twenty-three days and I wouldn't let him forget it. I brought it up time and time again just to annoy him when he was trying to check me on something.

"Well, let me go so I won't get sleepy on 85. I'll call you when I get home." He said while tapping on the steering wheel.

"Okay, be careful" before my left foot hit the ground he was at my side pulling me up "Dang, Johnnie on the spot, I can walk on my own." I said as I stood up.

"Come on girl it's getting late." He walked me to the door and gave me a hug and said "I'll see you tomorrow at church."

He strolled back to the car with his hands in his pockets. I stood in the doorway until he pulled away and as I cut the lights off and closed the door I heard something. I turned around to find my mom walking out of the darkness with her hands on her hips,

"You had a phone call." she said in an aggravated tone.

"Who was it, Joseph?" I asked trying to ignore the obvious disapproval.

"Yes. I told him you were out."

"What time was it when he called?" I asked.

"Around 11:00" she said sternly.

I glanced up at the clock and it was 2:00 a.m. my time.

"Okay thank you I'll call him." But she didn't move.

"Excuse me Momma."

She still stood there, so I just walked around her and made my way upstairs. I really wasn't in the mood for Round Two tonight. I slipped off my shoes and sat on the side of the bed. Should I call Joseph now or wait for Lamont to call first? If I call now when Lamont calls I'm going to have to ask him to hold while I answer his call. Then Joseph is going to want to know who's calling here this time of night. And on the flip side of that, if I answer Lamont's call while I'm on the phone with Joseph, when I tell Lamont goodnight he's going to want to know why I'm rushing off the phone. If I say I'm on the other line that's going to be another conversation. I decided to just wait until Lamont called and then I'd call Joseph.

"Eleven minutes: you are getting good at this," I commented instead of saying 'hello' as I answered Lamont's call. We talked for another two hours, like we hadn't just spent the night together, laughing the entire time. When we finally got off the phone I was too tired to call Joseph, so I figured I'd just hit him up tomorrow. He's probably at the club anyway. I rolled over to get in my favorite position and I saw my mom standing in my doorway. "We're going to have to talk about it one day," she said. "Whenever you're ready, I'm ready."

"Good night, momma; I love you." I pulled the covers over my head. I don't know how long she stood there because the next thing I knew it was 10:00 a.m. I sprang out of bed and scurried to the shower.

I'm not going to be late and give my mom an easy opening to start in on me today. Church was packed; it was a sea of variations of red as the church folks added their own style to represent Valentine's Day. I remember hearing pastor say that we focus too much on Philio, Eros and Ludis love and not enough on Agape love. I wonder what he was preaching about. I half-heartedly paid attention. I was too busy concentrating on staying awake.

It was as if there was a camera in my house. As soon as I stepped inside, the phone rang. "Hello, I see you finally made it in." Joseph said. He sounded annoyed.

"Well, hello, I'm fine and happy Valentine's Day to you, too." I shot back, too sleepy to argue with him right now.

"I called you last night but you weren't home," he continued. I guess he was going to let me know that he wasn't pleased.

"I know. My mom told me when I got in."

"So why didn't you call me back?" he questioned.

"It was late and I was tired, so I said I would call you today. What's with all the questions?" I was getting irritated.

"Nothing, don't worry about it." He sounded a little disappointed.

"What's with the attitude?" I redirected.

"I knew that you were sad that we couldn't be together for Valentine's Day so I went out of my way to make sure that I would be home for your birthday. That's the secret that I've been keeping for the past two weeks. That's why I've been so quiet I didn't want to spoil the surprise."

"That is so sweet; I can't believe you are going to be here for my birthday. I can't wait. When are you coming home?" I asked nearly squealing. I was too excited.

"March, 10 at 7:00 p.m., I can't wait to see you, babe"

"Me neither" I managed to gasp through my excitement. We talked a few moments more making major birthday plans, wished each other happy Valentine's Day and hung up the phone.

I forgot all about being sleepy. I had too much on my mind. I laid across the bed imagining how special my birthday was going to be, going over in my head what we were going to do. This went on for almost half an hour until the doorbell rang. I heard my mom call my name. I wonder who it is. I wasn't expecting anybody. As I started down the steps I saw Lamont standing there with some of the most beautiful rich red roses in his hand. Shock overcame me immediately. I definitely wasn't expecting him to bring me flowers. What was he thinking? Of course, my mom, his number one fan, was standing to his right almost blind because she was grinning so hard.

"Look what Lamont brought you," as if I couldn't see this 6'3 muscular man standing in the foyer.

"Yes I see. What is this about?" I asked as I raised my eyebrow.

"It is Valentine's Day. Don't most women get flowers from a man that cares about them?" he says as he extends his token of affection my way. I said 'Thank you' as I gave him a hug and walked towards the mantle to sit my roses down.

"He deserves more than that, give him a kiss or something" my mom suggested. A kiss? I'd never kissed him and I definitely wasn't going to do it standing in front of my mom!

"Go ahead. You can give him a little peck. It's not going to hurt anybody," she said as she was still grinning and pushed me towards him. So I closed my eyes, took a deep breath as I leaned my head back and… nothing. I had pecked him and felt nothing. I don't know what I was expecting, but there were no trimmers and my heart didn't putter. It was a harmless 'thank you' peck. For some reason that made me smile. I was relieved that I felt nothing but gratitude. We sat down to watch TV for a few minutes because it was almost time for him to head back to school. He ended up spending his last two hours with me so that I wouldn't be alone for Valentine's Day. See what I mean, he was such a thoughtful and caring man. I was so lucky to have him as a friend. His mom called and told him that his ride was on the way so he needed to head home. I gave him a big hug and watched him walk to the car as my mom stomped up to her room in defeat.

I ended up having the best Valentine's Day. I received some gorgeous flowers, hit a nice party, got to spend some quality time with my special friend and found out that Joseph would be here to bring in my birthday. A girl couldn't ask for anything better. My sister and I looked at bridal books until our eyelids won the fight and we slept the remainder of V-Day away!

Happy Birthday to me...

The next three weeks flew by and before I knew it I was standing at gate 14B at Charlotte Douglas International Airport, waiting for my man to exit the plane. I almost knocked an elderly couple over when I saw Joseph bop through the corridor. We hugged and kissed for what seemed like hours and then my sister cleared her throat. Once we regained our senses, he reached over and gave her a hug and we walked to the escalator to go claim his bags. My sister, Taz, was my trusty sidekick and my closest friend although we were six years apart in age. I was able to tell her some of my biggest secrets. Taz was the only one that knew Joseph was coming home; we were going to surprise everyone else. I had a small bag and Taz took his backpack while he struggled with the rest of his luggage.

"Why did you bring all of this?" I said. My curiosity was getting the best of me. "Because I'm going to be home for four weeks and then I'm going straight to Germany." I was speechless for a moment. So he was really coming home because he was going overseas and knew that he wouldn't be back for a while. And here I was thinking he was making a special trip just for me. Instantly, Lamont popped into my head. Did Joseph just say four weeks?

Taz looked at me and asked if everything was okay?

"I'm good. Just a little tired." I answered as I stared off into space.

"Babe do you mind driving? I've been driving all day." I asked ever so sweetly.

As he switched gears in Sent, my Black 1990 Nissan Sentra with the hot pink racing stripes on the bottom of the door, he and Taz cut up all the way to his house. I was sitting in the passenger seat doing some mental strategic planning. How am I going to get missing for 30 days? Damn it. If I had just told Lamont what was going on this wouldn't even matter. But no, I'd been so smart that now I'm the dummy. Well, I have to tell him now. There's definitely no way to hide this. I'll call him as soon as I get home. But in the mean time, it is good to see my man!

We clubbed it up that weekend. We hit Expressions, The Arena, and King Richards and my birthday wasn't until the following week. This was the Joseph I knew and loved. Always a bundle of fun. I would get off from work and go straight to his house. He would have a house full of his friends. His parents tolerated it because he only came home once a year. So what if a gang of young people took over the house for a few weeks, peace and quiet would return once his plane departed. I was like a leech my every free minute. His shadow came in second place. I was stocking up on together time because I wouldn't see him again until October.

I brought my wedding bag over so that he could see what I had selected. His response was "Just tell me when and where and what time; the rest doesn't matter to me." What kind of response is that? This was the beginning of the rest of our lives. How could he be so flippant about this? "What's up with that answer?" I said. "Do you want to get married or not? We don't have to get married, but I'll tell you this, I can't promise I'll be here when you get back." What the foolishness. Why did I even let that escape my mouth? No time to back track now so I threw the books and invitation samples in the bag and took them to my car. He followed me as I walked a mile a minute from the back of the house.

"Can you just wait a minute, please?" He yelled behind me as his boy Mike hollered out "Let her leave." I gave a quick, 'make it happen' glare and he recanted his statement while giving me a 'you know I was just playing' nudge of surrender. "It's not the time, Mike." Joseph said as we passed through the game room. When we reached the car my whole demeanor had changed.

"Baby, look we don't have to discuss it. That's not what this is about, but if you don't want to get married, now is the time to say it before any more time and money is invested." I truly meant that.

"That's not what I meant." Joseph said. "I was saying that I know you are going to pick something nice and you are better at planning than I am. Just tell us where to be and what time and everything is fine. That's all that meant, okay?" I smiled as I peered through his eyes trying to see his soul. I figured that I would be able to tell by his kiss- kisses don't lie. I leaned in and kissed him and just like that everything was fine.

I had to leave anyway not because I was mad but because he needed to spend some time with his friends alone. I'm sure they were tired of his girl tagging along and I needed to catch up with Lamont. He was coming home to take me out for my birthday and I hadn't even called to see when and where we were going.

"Lamont called you three times" my sister said as I walked in my room. Taz was just as bad as I was. She liked both of them and called them both her brothers.

"Lamont is waiting on you. I told him that you would be home by 6:00 so he said that he would be here by 7:00." She said as we ran up the stairs two at a time.

"But it's 6:15" I said frantically.

"I know. When I got off the phone with him I called over to J's house and they said that you were gone." She informed me while she was still on my heels.

"Yeah I had to ride around for a while to clear my head. I don't know if I'm coming or going right now" I sighed.

"I picked out something for you to wear, so go jump in the shower; time is ticking" she ordered.

I was thinking maybe I could take a rain check as the warm penetrating water ran down my body. Knock, knock, knock. My sister was banging on the door.

"D?"

"What?" I yelled hastily.

"Hurry up. Its 6:35 and Lamont just called. He's on his way."

Well there was no chance at a rain check. I had better get a move on. I got dressed as my mom and sister made a fuss over makeup, smell goods and all that jazz. I fastened my necklace and selected the perfect earrings and I was ready. Taz had selected this cute little cream and black outfit that Lamont gave me for Christmas. Of course he had good taste, look at his friend, I thought while striking a sexy pose in the mirror.

"D, you have company," my daddy yelled up the stairs. He continued with the small talk with Lamont until I entered the room; then he smiled. "Oh you're all dressed up. Where are you two going?"

"It's a surprise." Lamont said, pleased with himself.

"Well, we better get going" I said.

It wasn't that I was ready to go as much as I didn't want to get caught sitting in one place too long.

"What's the hurry?" Lamont said. His voice was a little too inquisitive for me so I reassured him that it was nothing and that I was just hungry. We were walking out the door when the phone rang. I paused for a brief moment and then commonsense took over and I quickly walked out the house.

"She just left" took the place of a goodbye as my daddy answered whoever was on the other end of the phone.

"We have time. You can get it if you want." Lamont suggested as he motioned towards the house.

So he was listening. "No, I'm good I can call whoever back when I get home." I answered as I continued walking towards the car. He opened the car door and waited for me to get situated before he closed it. As he walked around I leaned over and unlocked his side and then adjusted my seatbelt so that my outfit wouldn't get wrinkled.

"Where are we going" I asked as we headed out of the neighborhood.

"I told you it is a surprise" he replied. He was not giving up any information.

We pulled up to this elegant restaurant downtown. Whoa! He was really going over the top with this. When the valet opened the door and reached out his hand all I could think was 'I could get use to this.' I looked over at Lamont and said "You shouldn't have, but I'm glad you did. I've wanted to come here for as long as I can remember." I winked as I spoke, bursting with excitement.

"I know. I've heard you say it at least a million times. How could you not know that I was going to bring you here? You practically told me to." We gave a quick chuckle and regained control as we entered this exquisite dining room with the finest linens and antique china. It was illuminated by candlelight and the air was sweetened with the fragrance of fresh flowers. I knew this was going to be one of the best evenings of my life. We were all dressed up in one of the nicest restaurants we had ever been to and our vibe was in sync. It was as if we were the only two in the place and time had stopped and waited for us to relish in the moment.

"I don't think I want this night to end," I said. My Cinderella moment set in and I knew that my time was running out.

"Me either," he responded.

I was stunned that he felt the same way. Then we looked into each other's eyes as if for the first time and our hearts locked. I had to say something to break this up; it was getting too serious in here.

"I bet you don't because now it's time to pay." I said. I squeezed his hand and we started to laugh as the waiter brought him the supple leather bound folder with the receipt inside. I excused myself and went to 'powder my nose' while he took care of the particulars. I really just needed to get out of there so that I could check myself for a minute. I looked in the bathroom's mirror and replayed the evening in my head. What in the world is going on? Where is this going? I never meant to hurt him, ever. That was never my intention. I just enjoyed hanging with him and thought he was a nice guy. I never expected to have feelings like this for him and surely never thought I would fall in love with him. I shook my head violently as if I were fighting off a bad vision or something, freshened up my lips and walked out the ladies room.

When I got back to the table Lamont stood up and we walked out of the restaurant. As the maître d' opened the door there was a beautiful regal white horse-drawn carriage waiting just for us. I looked back at Lamont and then again at the carriage. It was all so breathtaking. But deep inside I knew that I didn't deserve all of this. I just stood there for a minute and then Lamont lead me by the hand down the stairs and into the carriage. We rode around downtown for at least an hour. It felt like we were the only people out that night and all of this was just for us to enjoy. I felt like the luckiest woman in the world. This night was magical in more ways than one. All of a sudden it was like my eyes were wide open and I could see everything clearly. I loved Joseph, but I was in love with Lamont. How could this be? How did I get here? My mind was spinning and my thoughts were suffocating me. I just closed my eyes, took a few deep breaths and whispered "Not tonight; the devil will not steal my joy tonight."

I got home, went straight to my room and shut the door. That lasted all of 30 seconds; Taz jumped into the bed beside me.

"So, how was it? What did you do?" she quizzed me, waiting for a play- by- play report. As I described the night to a T, not leaving out a single detail my sister sat straight up in the bed and started shaking her head. I stopped in mid sentence.

"What's your problem?" I asked.

"You love him, D. That's your problem and you are going to have to tell Joseph. He must already know something because he didn't even call while you were out." Ouch! That would have hurt under normal circumstances, but I hadn't given him two minutes of thought while I was out tonight. So no need to harp on it now, I'll tackle that later. When I finished telling of my fantasy come true my mom was standing at the door

"Oh no, not you, too," I said. Can I just have my perfect night without all the drama please?" I pleaded. "Just give me tonight and I'll figure out what I'm going to do later."

"You better start praying; that's what you better do," my mom replied as she walked away.

The phone rang and my sister and I looked at each other like it was a bomb or something. "You want me to answer that?" she asked.

"No. I got it." I answered as I inhaled some invisible courage and lifted the receiver.

"Hello?" I said. I was a little anxious this time because I didn't know whose voice was going to be on the other end and how I was going to react when I heard it. As I exhaled a sigh of relief Taz got up and yelled out "Hey, Lamont, I heard you did your thang tonight." She winked at me and smiled. She swears she knows who I'm talking to.

"Oh, I almost forgot, daddy said Moni called you right after you left" Taz added as she shut my room door on her way out.

I must have said 'thank you' a hundred times on the phone that night, but Lamont just kept playing it down as if it was routine to him and told me that I deserved it. *Mental note: I'm going to have to step my game up for his birthday after all of this. I can't imagine how he paid for all of tonight's activities.* He continued to tell me that the best part of the whole night was when he saw how my face lit up and that he was able to share it with me. How did I miss it? How could I have even doubted my feelings for him all of this time? I'm going to have a sit down with God and get some direction because right now I'm inapt. I don't know what I'm doing, where I'm going and, most importantly, who I'm supposed to be with?

I couldn't wait for this month to be over. I was going to have a heart attack before I turned 21. If I had to compare, then Lamont won hands down. But if I base it on effort put into the relationship, then Joseph would win. We'd been doing this for five or six years now. We knew all about each other- what made us tick, what made us happy, what we valued in life and not to mention he was my first true love. How did Lamont just come in and twist that all up in less than a year. If he could do that in that amount of time then surely I'm not ready. Nothing or no one should be able to come in and mess with my emotions like that. I was so confused I didn't know what to do.

My birthday came during the week and I spent it having dinner with my family and Joseph. My big gift from my parents was a beach trip at the end of the month. And although I had a ball that entire week, everything was minor in comparison to what Lamont had done. That was really special because he gave me exactly what I wanted- nothing more, nothing less. Now I was looking forward to going to the beach with my family, the getaway will do wonders for my mind. That will give me plenty of time to clear my mind and talk with God so when I come back, I will be completely focused.

It seemed as if it was only yesterday when I came home from the beach and Joseph just HAD to see me. Oh Lord what has he done? I knew he didn't wreck my car, which I had left for him to fix my brakes while I was out of town. He was too calm on the phone. He must have had sex with 'ole girl' from Atlanta. Whatever, this is it I'm tired of his mess (Over thinking) as usual. That was my specialty. So I set up shop on the stairs waiting for my Prince Charming to arrive.

Any and everything was racing through my head and as I sat there pondering over the unknown, the doorbell rang. When I opened the door a smile took over my face without warning. I just couldn't stay mad at him. After a long embrace my smile disappeared.

"What is it?" I demanded.

"Nothing," he said, "Just come with me." Now my man was fine. Handsome was an understatement. His eyes could break down any wall and his smile was so inviting. He had a good heart and a bubbly personality that was hypnotic. Not to mention a nice little frame. Yeah, I was just as lucky to have him, as he was to have me. So we're driving to his house and he has this stupid grin on his face that makes me sick. I continued to harass him trying to figure out what was going on. We have little conversation. (My man can't hold water), so as not to spoil the surprise he says nothing. When we get to the house his family is sitting there with the same silly grins. Now I'm really nervous. "What's going on?" I questioned cautiously.

We had just started planning our wedding. I know he's not going to call it off in front of his family; he could have done that at my house. I'm about to blank and... he kisses me. Okay now I know something is up, we usually don't have P.D.A. (Public Displays of Affection).

"What's with the smiles? You're scaring me now?" I said nervously.

"You are my whole world and I can't see me living without you"... I zoned out. I see his mouth moving, but he can't be saying what I think he's saying. What will my parents say? What does he mean this week? No I have to tell him I'm not ready yet. That I have some things to work on first. Did he just say Friday? But it's already Sunday night. How? Where? I don't get it. This isn't what we discussed three days ago. His lips stop moving, and I'm wondering why everyone is looking at me. I cracked under the pressure of hurting him. "Yes" I said. "Okay we can do it." That was the beginning of the 'perfect marriage.'

I'm asking myself how I could have said 'yes', knowing my situation. My daddy always told me, 'don't say what you won't do, because you'll end up doing it every time.' I just told him I will marry him and on Friday nonetheless. Only five days away. I didn't pray. I didn't think. I just reacted. Now that smile on my face is a mask for the mass confusion going on inside of me. What about Lamont? How can I tell him this? What about my family? What about me? The one thing I needed was the one thing that I had the least of... TIME!

The drive home from Joseph's was confusing. We had planned out the week and made a mental to-do list and now that was playing over and over in my head. The kiss goodnight was a reminder of what I had just done. As I walked in the house and closed the front door the phone rang. "Hey, babe did you have a nice time?"

That voice on the other end was melodic to my soul. This was the quiet before the storm. I've never lied to him before and I'm not about to start. Besides, he was just a friend. At least that's what I told myself. He was the one that I spent all my time with. He was the one who could comfort me when I was upset. He was the one that loved me for me and never held my imperfections against me. But isn't that what friends do? Everyone claims that we're more than friends, but

I tell them they just don't understand. Could it be that I'm the one that's lost? Lamont was the perfect gentleman- tall, dark, handsome, intelligent and, last but not least, a Christian. A woman couldn't ask for any more. But his timing was off. We had passed the 'more than friends' time limit. I was practically on my way down the aisle. How could I stop now? We talked for an hour or two, which was normal for us. But we never discussed that night, which was good for me. You don't ask I won't tell.

It's amazing how clear the night that Joseph proposed is in my head. And how, if I would have stepped back that night and just prayed and listened for God, I might not be signing these papers tonight. I enjoyed my life as a wife and I thought I was doing the right thing but in the end I learned that I did a grave injustice to a lot of people, including myself.

The next day I went to work, one of the best hiding places I had. Being a bus driver did have its perks. Neither one of them could reach me there. I had to go over to Joseph's during my morning break. I had no time to spare. I had to pick him up, drive to York, SC, about a half an hour south of Charlotte. We planned to apply for a marriage license there, since we could get married faster in South Carolina, and make it back to Charlotte before 1:00.

When I pulled into his driveway I could see Joseph waiting in the game room. I watched him as he walked towards the passenger side door and let him in the car. He was preoccupied, but I didn't have time to drill him. I had a lot more on my plate. At least his family knew. I still hadn't found the courage to tell mine. And I've talked to Lamont but those words never crossed my lips. I hadn't even told my sister and the rest of The Foundation yet.

Army regulations were putting a snag in our plans. I was still trying to grasp these new stipulations.

"Okay do I understand this right; per military regulations we can't be put on the housing list until we're married?" I asked still wrestling with our new plan.

"Yes D, that's what I told you last night." Joseph snapped.

"Well excuse me!" I answered sharply. "You don't have to bite my head off."

"I'm sorry, baby. It's just that I didn't get much sleep last night.

That's all. I'm just a little tired."

"Grouchy, too, if you ask me but I forgive you. I have to make sure that I know what I'm talking about when I tell my parents. You know they are going to have a million questions." I sighed as a vision of the inquisition played out in my mind.

"That's what I was thinking about last night when you left. You don't have to tell them. We can get married. I will take the certificate to Germany and put our name on the list. Then in October I will come back, we'll have our wedding and then we're off to start our new life together. It would be like this one never happened." He smiled nervously as he explained the scenario.

"Really? I like that option better. That way no one will get hurt, especially me" I exhaled, we laughed and just like that everything was cool. This week was more of a technicality than anything else. October would still be our real wedding.

We were in and out of the magistrate's office with time to spare. I can't believe that's all we had to do to get a marriage license. They make it so easy. All that was left for us to do was to come back on Friday and pick up the license and make the arrangements with the judge. The courthouse gave us a recommendation on which judge to use. I called him when we got back to Charlotte and set the time for Saturday at 9:30 in the morning. This wedding was too simple. We didn't even need a witness. The judge's wife will be our witness. Everything was happening so fast and with ease, it was almost scary.

All of the loose ends were taken care of. All I had to do now was show up. Why couldn't my real wedding be that easy? The cost and the plans were overwhelming me. My mom was helping now but my heart wasn't in it like before. I found myself thinking more and more about Lamont. I couldn't find the words to tell him that I cared about him, but I'm getting married and leaving the country. That didn't even sound right? The stress of the betrayal was getting the best of me.

The Foundation was picking out their bridesmaids dresses, but I was in my own world. They could have pranced in front of me in burlap sacks right now and I wouldn't have noticed. 'I'm getting married on Saturday' is what I wanted to holler out, but my voice was paralyzed by fear. I guess as long as I was saying it to Joseph it was fine. But to say it to someone else makes it seem real and I'm not sure if I'm ready to accept my reality yet.

The closer it got to Friday the more I thought of Lamont. How could I hurt someone like that? I never meant for it to go this far. How can I be woman enough to say 'I do' and not be woman enough to tell Lamont that I'm getting married Saturday? He deserves to know. I'm sure there's a woman at school that would love to have his heart. I mean who wouldn't? If I were in a position to, I would. I just keep replaying what Lamont said about loving two people and all I can do is close my eyes and shake my head in self disgust. I really did it this time.

"What about this dress, D?" Taz asked, while modeling a selection as she finally got my attention.

"Yeah that's a nice one; do all of you like it?" I questioned, trying to seem involved.

"If we didn't we wouldn't have tried it on," Taz, the great detective, said. "You haven't been any help today. What's up?"

"Nothing really; just tired. You know I really haven't had any rest since Joseph has been home. Sad to say, but I'm sort of looking forward to Sunday." I shrugged my shoulders and cut my eyes over towards them to poll their responses.

"I bet you are, but it doesn't have anything to do with Joseph leaving. It's really because you haven't been able to hang out with Lamont" Taz was so sure of herself and her announcement. We all laughed.

"Whatever, chick. I really like that dress. How much is it?" I quizzed, using my secret weapon, the infamous change of subject, so I didn't have to say she was right.

"They're actually on sale, but we have to buy them by the end of the month," Rochelle said.

"Can you all handle that?" I said. I surveyed my girls as I scanned the room for the sales attendant.

"We'll see," they chimed in unison.

"Well, we have the dresses taken care of; let's go get something to eat. What do you have a taste for?" I rubbed my stomach like I had worked up an appetite.

The Waffle House won, as usual. I needed this time with my girls. Taz and Moni were acting up as always. They are so crazy. Kira and Rochelle were having their own conversation, so I was able to take some time out of my relationship mayhem and enjoy the moment. We vowed to spend more time together, especially since I'm leaving in October. I'm really going to miss them. I wish they could go with me. That would be the chance of a lifetime, to have a little piece of home in Germany with me.

"There's a party Saturday, do you want to go?" Saturday! I had almost forgotten about Saturday. "Sorry, I can't make it. That's Joseph's last night at home." I answered, with an apologetic smile on my face. What I really should have said is that that's my wedding day so I don't think that I'll be free Saturday. They would freak out!

This week was flying by. I have to get a move on. Friday came before I knew it. We have to go pick up the license and I need to get back so that I can go to work. I go scoop Joseph up and we grab a bite to eat and hit I-77 south. We listened to Power 98 on the radio and they are really jamming today. We talk about how nice it's going to be when I get to Germany. I have heard so much about it from my parents. We were stationed over there when my daddy was in the Army, so this will be my second time around. I don't remember anything about my first trip, but I've seen some pictures. I think it will be cool to see the places where my parents and I used to live and visit, as well as creating some new memories of our own.

As we pulled in the parking lot, I got this weird feeling, but attributed it to nerves. We held hands as we climbed the stairs, but said nothing. It was almost like we wanted the other to say 'I changed my mind,' but we didn't say a word. Once the clerk located our license and Joseph paid the fee we were on our way home. Now the ride back was silent. I leaned my seat back and took a nap while Joseph took us up the highway listening to Tupac. When we pulled up to the house, I popped up like a jack-in-the box. I had 15 minutes to make it to work. I gave Joseph a quick peck and I was on my way.

Every possible thought rushed through my head. I was shaking with fear and excited at the same time. Why am I'm feeling like this? I was going to do it in six months anyway. Maybe these were the wedding jitters that every bride gets. I'll be fine tomorrow. I made it to work with seconds to spare and it was back to business no questions asked.

I spent my last "single lady" Friday night at Joseph's house. Ma, Joseph's stepmother, cooked, we ate dinner, then played video games and listened to music for the rest of the night. It was getting late and we had to get up early in the morning so I headed home. Once I was in the house, I tipped up the stairs and laid across my bed to relax. I had a big day ahead of me tomorrow. I had better get some rest.

I woke up to Taz yelling my name and telling me to get the telephone.

"If you didn't want to do it that's all you had to say" Joseph said, in lieu of good morning.

"What are you talking about?" I mumbled, still half sleep and confused.

"It is 9:00 D. We aren't going to make it in time." Joseph did not mask the anger in his voice.

"Calm down, I forgot to set my clock. Let me jump in the shower and I'll be there. I already know what I'm wearing I'll be there by 9:30." Neither one of us believed that. A quick shower for me is 15 minutes. The earliest I would make it there is 9:45, but my response seemed to pacify him temporarily. I called the judge and told him that we were running late and asked could we still come? He confirmed that he didn't have another wedding until 11:00, so if we made it before then he would still be able to perform the ceremony.

While in the shower panicking because I couldn't believe I'd over slept my sister slid in the bathroom with her 50 questions.

"Where are you two going? Why was he so upset?" This girl should be a blame investigation detective.

"What are you doing up so early" I asked.

"I couldn't sleep because Joseph kept calling. I finally said 'let me wake her up' and that's when I came in your room. You must have really been tired you still had your clothes on. You still didn't say where you two are going?" I just closed my eyes and took a deep breath I had no explanation so I said nothing. Just as she was going to start in again my mom called her downstairs for breakfast. Thank you, Lord. I didn't know what I was going to say if she would have asked again. I was out of the house in record time, add the seven minutes it takes to get to his house and I was pulling in his driveway at 9:50. When I walked in the house his family was eating breakfast. Everything looked good but I didn't have an appetite or the time so I passed on the invite. He still had an attitude when I walked in his room. We didn't have time for all of this, so I just listened as he put on his shoes. As we were leaving Ma whispered that she bet she knew where we were going as we headed towards the back door. When we got in the car I apologized at least three times for oversleeping. At first he acted like he was mad, but when he saw that I was getting pissed, he gave in.

We didn't have much to say on the way down, but my heart was pounding. I was really nervous and I couldn't believe we were doing it! As Joseph read off the directions to the judge's house the mood got lighter and we finally had smiles on our faces. I was rolling down the highway. We arrived at the judge's house in about 30 minutes. We pulled into this gravel driveway of a beautiful stone home with a perfectly manicured lawn. From the outside you would never have guessed that this has been the locale for so many nuptials. This cute little middle-aged couple greeted us at the door.

"We thought you had gotten cold feet" the judge chuckled.

"One of us almost did," Joseph said. He had managed to sneak one in on me. I cut my eye at him but never lost my smile. The judge asked for the license and he and his wife signed and then they asked us if we were ready. We gave each other a quick look and said 'yes.' The judge even threw a joke in about my parents hiding in the trunk. Joseph said "I hope not", and we all laughed. Five minutes later I was saying those two words every woman dreams of "I do."

Just Another Day...

We got back to Charlotte by noon and I was exhausted. We went to my house. We took our wedding bands off, placed them in the ring box and got out of the car like nothing had happened. My daddy and uncle were outside when we pulled up. When we walked in the house my mom was sitting at the kitchen table on the phone and Taz was watching TV in the den. Joseph and I collapsed on the sofa and immediately fell asleep. We awoke to the telephone ringing. It was after 5:00 and my house was empty. The answering machine was picking up when I heard Lamont's voice. I'm surprised I didn't give Joseph whiplash moving his head off my lap and running to catch the phone.

"Hello, hold on let me cut the machine off" I said while panting.

"Where have you been; I've been calling you?" he said.

"I've been busy what's up?" I retorted.

"Nothing. I hadn't talked to you in a while. Is everything alright?" I could hear the curiosity in his voice.

"Yes, what's up?" I was trying to ward off any questions he may have and gain control of the conversation.

"I was going to come over. What are you getting into?"

"Oh, I was just leaving. Maybe tomorrow. What time are you going back?" I asked softly "8:00 at the latest," he said, obviously disappointed that he wouldn't see me tonight.

"That would be better for me." I said. "I'll give you a call when I get home." I really didn't want to see him tonight for fear of what I would feel. Besides he didn't need to pop up over here right now.

That would be all bad. He knew Joseph was home but he had no intentions of meeting him and I definitely didn't oppose. I woke Joseph up and we headed for his house.

Joseph still had to pack and get everything in order because we had to leave for Atlanta by 9:00 the next morning. Moni and Richard were riding with me so I didn't have to drive back by myself. I hate 'goodbyes', so I really didn't feel like being over here tonight. Joseph packed our marriage license with a copy of his orders and placed them in his backpack. I just sat and looked as he was getting his stuff together. He kept touching my head and telling me that everything is going to be alright. "October will be here before you know it and we'll have the wedding that you want and everything will be fine." I just nodded my head and helped him pack his bags. I couldn't wait until I could stop hiding this from my family and friends. It didn't seem fair that his people knew and mine were in the dark.

I was focusing more on how my decision was going to affect Lamont than Joseph leaving in the morning. I was second-guessing myself, and that was bothering me. It's not like October wasn't coming. I was going to walk down the aisle any way. Could someone please explain these feelings that I'm having? I've got to tell Lamont tomorrow. He deserves to know the truth and evidently I'm not going to have any peace until I share my secret with him. How was I going to look him in the eyes and tell him that I'm someone else's wife? If there was a way that I could evade this conversation I would, but life couldn't be that easy!

I told Joseph that I needed to go home to get some rest for the trip in the morning but really I just wanted to sleep my confusion away. 7:00 a.m. came quickly and I was up again. I took my shower and was getting dressed when my daddy came in the room to find out where I was going this time of morning. When I said that I was taking Joseph to Atlanta to catch his plane, WWIII began!

I didn't understand what the big deal was. I wanted to see him off and someone was going with me so I wasn't going to be alone on the way back. Out of the corner of my eye I could see my mom making her way to my room and 'it was on.' They were going full speed ahead now! I would get a word in every now and then, but for the most part it was their show.

I finished getting dressed and rushed out of the room. They followed me down the stairs and to the front door. That's when the standoff began. I was determined to go and they were going to make sure that I didn't. After about 15 minutes my daddy lost interest, threw up his hands and told me to do whatever I wanted to do he didn't care anymore. Now he was going too far. It wasn't that serious. I wanted to scream 'he's my husband,' but I chickened out. When I reached over to kiss my parents "bye" they were like emotionless statues. I hated to leave like this, but I had a long drive ahead of me. I told them that I loved them and shut the door. A tear rolled down my face. I was choosing between the people that I loved the most. I had to believe that I was doing the right thing. I sat in the car for a minute and cried in peace. I felt like I was being pulled in three directions trying to please everyone and I was fed-up.

I finally pulled off. My cry was a momentary fix to a hectic situation that I was going to have to handle. If I had just been honest with everyone this wouldn't even be an issue. My parents would understand me taking my husband to the airport. If this is any indication of my next six months then heaven help me. I turned the music up to drown out my thoughts. I even slept through a light or two in route, but I needed that time to get myself together.

When I pulled up at Moni's house her parents were in rare form, too. What in the world is going on this Sunday morning? To satisfy her parents, we ended up taking Ray, Moni's younger brother, along on our trip. For what we couldn't figure out, since he couldn't help drive. He was only taking up space. But if that's the only way that Moni could go then I guess we didn't have a choice.

We pulled up to Joseph's house and his bags were in the driveway. He and Richard, his older brother and partner in crime more times than I care to remember, were waiting inside. We loaded up the car and he said his 'goodbyes' and we were off. As soon as we drove off the mood changed and there was a feeling of peace. I don't know if it was because for at least eight hours I wouldn't have to deal with my drama or because, if only for one day, happiness was acceptable, even with all the deception.

Atlanta was an easy drive straight down I-85 south and we were at the airport in no time. We set up camp at his departure gate and prepared for the unyielding wait until it was time to board the plane. We joked about the past month's activities and made all of these plans for his October trip home. Richard pulled Joseph over to the bar to have a good-bye drink and to discuss some things that I wasn't supposed to know about, I'm sure.

As they walked off Moni asked me if we had gotten married and didn't tell anyone. I smiled and asked her why she asked me that. She just said she had that feeling. I never answered her. I started talking about the wedding plans that still needed to be taken care of. We still had to find some shoes and I figured that we could stop by a couple of stores in Atlanta after Joseph boarded the plane.

The wait felt longer than it actually was, but before we knew it we were hugging and saying 'good-bye.' I know we embraced five times and it was then that we realized he was one of the last people left to board the plane. I felt like a part of me was leaving when they closed the boarding door of the airplane. Moni hugged me as I stared out the window with my hand pressed against the glass. We stayed there until the plane was out of sight. I wiped a stream of tears from my face and we walked towards the car in silence.

Once we closed the doors Richard assured me that everything was going to be alright and asked where we wanted to eat. We pulled out of the parking lot and decided to just head on home. I snoozed while Moni and Richard drove. As soon as we hit the Charlotte city limits my body could tell. I couldn't get comfortable anymore. It was amazing. It seemed like the stress had given me a 'day pass' and waited anxiously for my return. After everyone was dropped off, I headed home. I glanced at the clock and saw that it was after 8:00. Good, Lamont has left for the week. I can get a good night sleep and come up with a game plan for telling him what was going on. I pulled into the driveway and all the lights were off. This was perfect. I would be sound asleep by the time my family got home. I ran in the house and checked the answering machine. No messages…good.

I may have made it up to the fourth step when the phone rang. I ran to my room and caught it by the end of the second ring. It was Lamont.

"Hey, I see you're at home. I was going to stop by since we aren't leaving until later. My ride had something to do so we are just going to leave out early in the morning."

I looked to heaven for mercy and just shook my head. "I'm here".

He hung up and was at my door in 10 minutes flat, breaking his own record. I opened the door and walked away. He shut the door and walked over and sat on the sofa. He looked, smiled and asked what I had been up to. Why wasn't I in church today and why was I so tired? I told him that I had taken Joseph to Atlanta to catch his plane. He didn't respond at first. I almost thought he didn't hear me but then he opened and extended his arms and I leaned in as he gave me a big hug. He lifted my chin with his finger and assured me that I was going to be alright. Then he asked who went with me, making sure that I didn't go alone. Was I hearing him correctly? Was he really that concerned about me? Wow, he's a bigger person than I am. I wouldn't have cared one bit, but that's what makes him so special. That's a true friend.

We talked a little while and then I stretched out across his lap and went to sleep. We may have been sleep 30 minutes when my parents came in and woke us up. I walked him to the car and said goodnight and walked back in the house. I didn't even wait for him to pull off tonight. I went up stairs and was sleep before the room got dark. This has been one of the longest most stressful months of my life and it had taken its toll on me. I slept through the morning. It was afternoon when I finally opened my eyes. I took a deep breath and rolled out of bed. The house was empty; good I needed some me time. I laid in the bed and flicked through the channels, then I took a shower, talked on the phone with my girls for a little while and dozed off again. When I finally woke up my family was home. I could hear them downstairs laughing and talking. I was going to miss them when I left. I tried to imagine how my new life was going to be. I was going to have to make new friends and I would miss the holidays and family gatherings. Lord, I pray I did the right thing. I decided to call it a night, so I set my alarm, closed my eyes, exhaled and whispered 'I love you' to my family as I visited "la-la" land yet again.

It was business as usual the following day. I went to work and on my break I went to school. The phone rang as soon as the thought of rest crossed my mind. It was Joseph letting me know that he made it and how he had signed in at his barracks and signed up for housing.

"Guess what babe I got us a place", I could hear the excitement in his voice. I know he didn't just say what I think he said.

"How did you get a place that fast? What happened to the six months?" I scoffed. I knew we shouldn't have lied, I just felt that something was going to go wrong.

"You are going to have to tell your parents because a lady is going to be calling you and sending you some papers with my name on them." He paused.

"How in the world did this happen? Can't we still just wait until October when you come home and I can leave with you?" I was panicking.

"No. They are going to send you some orders and you have to report here by September 10th"

I was floored! I cannot believe he is saying this. I am so done with him at this point that I'm ready to get off the phone.

"I'm sorry, Babe. I know you don't want to tell your parents like this. But it's the only way. They are going to find out one way or the other." He was speaking Greek to me. I just shook my head and slowly moved my hand up and down my face.

"I love you and I'll call you on Friday," he said, waiting for my reply.

"Bye" I said with no enthusiasm.

I just wanted to run away. A grown woman running from her problems. That's just the desperation taking over. I was woman enough to marry him, so I have to be brave enough to tell my family. Who should I tell first? I need some allies. Sadly, no one came to mind. Everyone was going to have something to say and I can't imagine any of it being positive.

I was so overwhelmed that I couldn't catch my breath. I tried to regain my composure before someone came in and demanded to know what was wrong with me. My head was pounding like I had been in a train wreck and my breathing was labored. I kept having anxiety attacks and needed to get some fresh air. I didn't talk much that night or the next night, for that matter. I was too afraid. Afraid of what I was going to hear from the people that I loved the most.

I had figured that by October they would have warmed up to the idea and would have been more open about the wedding. But this wasn't going to go over well at all. Oh Lord, now I really have to tell Lamont. He's going to hate me. I just know it. What have I done?

THE phone call came on Friday. My military transition counselor talked for about fifteen minutes straight without interruption. I took notes as she told me what was needed and by what date. She told me that my packet should arrive any day. She made sure that I didn't have any question before she finished up the conversation. "Congratulations" was the last thing she said as we got off the phone. Great! Now I have to meet the mailman every day. This is just too much work. The package arrived on Tuesday. Thankfully, my mom had something to do and I beat her home from work. I read through everything and looked at the orders. To see September 10th in black and white made it official for me. Lamont called while I was reading over the papers and that's when it hit me- his birthday was September 8th. What was I going to do? If I could just make it until his birthday, then I would be happy. That may not even be an issue after I tell him that I'm married. He may never want to see me again.

Lamont and I had a one sided conversation today. He did all the talking and I just gave 'yes' and 'no' answers when prompted. My withdrawn state bothered Lamont but he didn't want to be too intrusive. He asked was there anything that he could do and when I told him 'no', he let it go. He started making jokes to brighten my spirits. I resisted at first but he had skills. He could always make me smile. We talked about everything, yet nothing of importance, and for a brief moment those orders didn't exist.

Once we were off the phone I started filling out this mountain of paper work. I had to go get a passport picture taken to submit with my application and mail it in by next week. That was going to be a problem since I hadn't changed my name on anything. I read over the list of acceptable ID documents and saw that I could use my marriage license. I'll do that first thing in the morning and get it in the mail since it takes a while to do the background check.

I had been spending a lot of time by myself since Joseph left. The only person that I could talk to was his mom. I would call and talk to her for hours. She even volunteered to be there with me when I told my family. I told her that was okay. Honestly, I didn't think that was going to be a good idea. There was no telling what my family was going to say. I had been rehearsing my spill. I was going to have the answer to every question that they could possibly ask. I played it over and over again in my mind and I had everything under control. At least that's how it played out in my head. I was thinking I would do it at my sister's birthday party since everyone would be at the house.

This can't be real...

My mom came in and asked me to ride over Nana's with her so I grabbed my sandals and walked outside. I said that I would drive so we wouldn't have to switch out cars. We were gone for a while. Nana, my momma's mother, was extra entertaining today. I must admit that was the most fun Momma and I had had in months. We were on our way home when this mad man pulled out in front of us and I had to slam on breaks.

"What's that?" my mom asked. Something had slid from under my seat.

"I don't know. Let me see what it is?" I had completely forgotten about my little escapade. I asked her to pick it up and as soon as she touched it I knew what it was... that blame marriage license.

My mom started shaking and asked me what it was. My first instinct was to lie, so I told her it was a fake. Then she asked me to look her in the eye and tell the truth and I crumbled.

"It's not what you think." I said.

Tears streamed down my mother's face and I couldn't get her home fast enough. I was in striking distance you know. I didn't like being the cause of my mother's tears; I had done that enough as a teenager. I thought that I had grown out of that stage. When we pulled up my daddy was under the hood of the van. My mom got out of the car and slammed the door. My daddy looked up, wondering what was going on. This isn't going to be good I thought.

"Your daughter has something to tell you," my mom said and stormed into the house. I knew she was upset, but couldn't she at least wait until we went in the house.

"What's going on Stuff?" my daddy asked as he rubbed his forehead. I just stood there dazed looking at him for a moment and then asked him to come in the house. Once my sister joined us in the den I slowly began to talk.

"Well, this isn't how I wanted to tell you but…"

"She's married" my mom blurted out.

"For real" my sister said. She stood and stretched her arms out to me and smiled. She was the only one of the bunch. My daddy must have been in shock because he didn't bat an eye as he stared through me. He started crying and shaking his head. I tried to say it as I had rehearsed over and over again but it wasn't working. Every time I looked like I was going to say something, my parents told me to shut up. The shouting match went on and on and I just sat there. I could just kill Joseph was all that was running through my mind. He had to know ahead of time that it wasn't going to take that long to get housing. He tricked me because he didn't want to have a wedding.

Out of nowhere my daddy said "Stuff, you didn't have to sneak off and get married. You were planning on doing it in October any way. So that's why you made such a big deal out of going to Atlanta. He was your husband. It all makes sense now."

Then the house was quiet. I never meant for it to be children against parents. Finally I broke the silence. "Listen the only reason we did it this way was is because you have to be married to be on the housing list. We were still going to have the wedding and then go to Germany. I didn't mean to hurt anyone. That was never my goal. I'm sorry and I hope that you forgive me." My sister and I turned and walked out the den.

The rest of the night was like a broken record. My mom would call a relative and say the same thing: "Guess who's married. Divine." Then she would call for me to pick up the phone and I would get blasted by yet another loved one. I never realized how many of them were against us getting married. They all basically said the same thing: "I can't believe you did that. You took that special moment from us." When I would try and explain they would just talk over me. By the fifth call I gave up. I remember my uncle saying that if I was happy he was happy, but he just hated the way we did it. I never looked at eloping as a bad thing; it was just the quickest way to get it done. That night was a new beginning. At least now I didn't have to lie anymore and now I can start getting my stuff together.

My sister's birthday was more about me than necessary. My family looked at me like I was the featured act for the freak show at the fair. The disappointment dampened the mood a bit but I could handle it. I had formed my alliance now. I was ready for whatever they threw my way. As luck would have it, it ended up being the children against the parents. Although they said it was out of love they used some pretty abrasive words and gave some harsh examples, so I would have to beg to differ. After a couple of rounds I rallied my troops and we took a walk. The parents were wearing me down. I was fighting a losing battle. It wasn't like I could shut them up, married or not. I would have gotten my head knocked off and I was getting tired of talking about the situation. It was already done.

I was glad to find that my marriage wasn't at center stage when we got back. Now there was someone else…Lamont. Evidently he had called while I was out and my mom couldn't wait to let me know when we walked up in the yard. I had been avoiding his calls for about a week for lack of the words to say and he was not pleased.

"He's on his way over here," my mom said as I stepped in the house.

"Over where?" I asked. I really didn't want to tell him with my audience captivated by our every word. I had to think quickly. I figured that I would just call him and tell him to meet me at the bowling alley. We would all hang out; no harm no foul.

Before I could even dial one digit the doorbell rang. I could have died right then and there. Knowing how my family was I took off for the door. My feet may have touched the floor every other step as I leaped for the knob. I headed him off telling him that we were going bowling and everyone was ready. I asked if he was hungry and lead him into the kitchen so that he could fix a plate. My mom came in and grabbed his hand and escorted him out to the den of wolves. I was right on his heels; I was not going to let him find out like that. My mom introduced him to the ones that didn't know him with the "this is the one I was telling you about" phrase. Lamont was smiling showing all 32 teeth. I could just shake him, thinking 'don't fall for her game.' I knew my mom wouldn't do anything to hurt Lamont but she was definitely going to use it as ammunition later.

After Lamont finished with his plate my sister, cousins, Lamont and I all headed out for the bowling alley. We had so much fun. If each pin represented an adult I should have bowled a perfect game the way I was feeling. I couldn't be mad at anyone but myself though. I was the one that had let this go on for all this time. I did have every opportunity to let him know, but instead I ran from my responsibilities as a friend. I didn't even deserve to use that word right now. I wasn't acting like a friend. A real friend would have told him what was going on. It was hard for me to look at him, because when I did all of these feelings would show themselves and I was finding it harder and harder to convince myself that I just loved him as a friend. It was getting late and all of us were tired and ready to go so we loaded up the cars and headed for the house. When we got home everyone was pulling out so I guess we timed that perfectly.

After the last car had pulled off, Lamont and I sat and looked at the stars and talked. It was almost summer break for him. He was really looking forward to coming home but had to take a class in summer school because they weren't going to offer it next year. That worked in my favor. We wouldn't be able to spend a lot of time together and that would make it easier when it was time for me to leave. Lamont looked at me with concern in his eyes. He asked me if I had something to say that he needed to know? I couldn't believe my ears. I had made sure that my mom didn't have time to even whisper anything to him. How could he know?

"What makes you say that?" I said. I hoped he couldn't sense the nervousness in my voice. "You just haven't been yourself lately," he replied.

"I've just been busy that's all." Thankfully, that seemed to hold him off. We sat listening to the radio and singing along to pass the time. I said everything but what I needed to say that night. How easy it would have been to just tell him and get it over with. But I still wasn't ready.

Going somewhere...

Time started flying by, it's already August. It was time to get our household items because the military was going to come and pick them up in two weeks. I couldn't decide on what to get, especially since I didn't know what the place looked like. I was shopping in the blind. I had my mom in every furniture store I could think of. She had now become my shopping buddy. She decided that the little time that we had left together should be happy. We looked for curtains, entertainment centers, dinette sets and whatever else we could think of. Joseph sent some money to buy everything but he wasn't very helpful with letting me know what we needed and didn't need. My family was going to have me a going away party/reception and everyone was going to give a gift to help us get started.

I finally decided on the big items and had them delivered to the house three days before everything was to be shipped. It was going to be pretty cramped for the weekend. The government couldn't pick the items up until Monday so it was going to have to sit in the living room and foyer until then. By Sunday we had piled it all up as neatly as possible and had it boxed and labeled by rooms to make it easy on myself when it was time to unpack.

My mom and I were sitting downstairs watching TV when the doorbell rang. We looked at each other because we weren't expecting company, plus neither of us wanted to miss any of the show we were watching. My sister went to answer the door after we didn't budge but reconsidered when she saw who it was. She peeped around the corner and motioned for me to come in the living room. I knew right then it was Lamont.

No, he can't find out like this! I wonder why he hadn't called. My mom grabbed my arm and said, "You are going to have to tell him. The longer you wait the worst it's going to be on him." I nodded 'yes,' but in my mind I was saying 'not tonight.' I walked over, opened the door and gave him a long, firm embrace. I wish that he would overlook all of the boxes and furniture, but he was not having it.

"What's all this," he asked, while admiring my good deals.

"My furniture," I answered nonchalantly.

"Oh, we're moving?" he asked. There was a touch of sarcasm in his voice since this was the first he had heard of it.

"Yes," I responded. I went and sat down and Lamont started playing with entertainment center.

"Hey, Mrs. Hill," he said.

"This is nice. Your place is going to be real nice, I see. You can't live like the rest of us college students."

The smirk on his face told me we were playing go fish. I never said anything about school, but if that's what he wanted to think that's fine. I really didn't want to open that can of worms tonight.

My mom walked out of the den, but not before she could mouth a threat letting me know that I had better tell him and she meant it. I sat motionless, but was praying the entire time, "Lord, if she doesn't go upstairs I'm going to die." That's about all I could get out before the phone rang. With the way my luck was going I'd bet anything it was Joseph. One, two, three... "D, telephone" my sister yelled down the stairs.

"I win," I blurted out of nowhere as I walked towards the kitchen. Even though it felt like I walked a mile to get to that phone, I had to force myself to take a breath once I had the receiver in my hand. It was times like this that I hated this new phone. Our cordless phone was broke and my mom had replaced the phone with a phone with a cord which meant there was nowhere to run!

Joseph greeted me with "Hey, baby I miss you," once I picked up the phone. Oh boy, it's going to be one of these conversations. I had better go upstairs.

"Hey, hold on one minute. I'm going to have to go upstairs. I can barely hear you." I called for Taz to pick up the phone in my room.

I placed the kitchen phone back on the hook, told Lamont I'd be right back and took off upstairs. My mom almost clothes lined me in mid-stride, "I'm not playing with you, tell him," she said. I managed to escape and shut my door, (which could have gone either way. We keep an open door policy around here. It's completely understood that Taz and I don't own doors, so we keep them open most of the time). My mom let it go tonight and I was glad.

I picked up the receiver and spoke to my husband. "Okay, I'm back. How are you doing?" I asked, but not really focused enough to care one way or the other.

He answered with "I miss you," sounding like he was waiting for my reply.

"I miss you too and I can't wait until I get there. What's the weather like? Have you found me a hairstylist yet? Did you stop some ladies with nice hairdos and ask them who their stylist was, like I asked?" I said all of this in one breath. I'm sure I blindsided him with this mini pop quiz but I needed to know.

"I haven't had time plus there's a hair salon at the PX. The PX is the military's version of an on base department store where only military families can shop. You have three years here. You'll find someone. Trust me. So when are you coming? The neighbors are starting to wonder if there really is a 'Mrs.' " Joseph said.

"I get there on the 10th, do you need to know my flight number or my gate?" I questioned.

"I'll get that later, I just wanted to call and tell you goodnight and to let you know that I was missing you and I love you," he responded.

That made me smile. "I love you too, goodnight!" I hung up the phone and waited for a minute, releasing a sigh of relief. I checked the clock and realized that I had been upstairs for about 10 minutes. I headed back to the den not really knowing what to expect. I found Taz and Lamont sitting there in tears laughing about something. Whew! That was close. I'm glad he's in a good mood. I wanted to be in on the private joke.

"What's going on; what's so funny?" They both just looked at me and laughed some more. I just shook my head and told them how silly they were and went and grabbed a snack. This only made it worst. Then I realized that I was the center of the joke.

"Yum-Yum, are you straight" and then more laughter. They were beginning to bug me, but then I had to laugh at myself. I had been snacking the entire time that Lamont had been there and I didn't even notice. It must have been my nerves.

We watched TV and joked around for a little while until Lamont just had to know. He looked me dead in my eyes and asked, "So where are you moving to and why didn't you tell me?"

"I didn't think it mattered," was all I could say.

"What is that supposed to mean; why wouldn't it matter?" His voice was getting a little deep and Taz figured now was as good a time as any to make her exit. She told Lamont that she would catch him the next time and walked upstairs. She peered back at me as she hit the corner with this pitiful look on her face. She was a traitor. She crumbled under the pressure. She knew it was about to get nasty in here and she didn't want any part of it. I turned to her with my eyes begging her to take me with her because I didn't want to do what I knew I had to do.

Lamont fussed for a few minutes about respect and how friends treat each other. Then there was only silence for several minutes. I didn't know how to start. I cleared my throat at least twice but no words came out. I was speechless, which doesn't happen too often.

He gave me a hug and said that he was getting tired and was about to go home. I guess he had had enough of me for one night. I hugged him longer than I normally did. I was trying to gather the courage to tell him that I was going to Germany, but I just couldn't do it. I was too afraid of him hating me. I told him to call me when he got home. He told me not to wait up. I knew then that he was mad as I walked him to the door. He looked at my furniture and then back at me and shook his head. I knew that I had disappointed my friend and there was no way that I could make that up to him.

I felt so low. I just sat in the bed and replayed the past year over and over, trying to figure out how I ended up in this predicament. A tear rolled down my cheek and I quickly wiped it away. I didn't deserve to cry. I was the one that created this mess and I deserved to feel all the pain I was experiencing. I didn't know how to fix this problem. This wasn't just about me. I was hurting someone who loved me with all his heart. The worst part of it all was that he still didn't know that I was married and that I was moving to Germany. I had two weeks to figure out how I was going to tell him.

I started packing clothes to block my thoughts and keep me busy. I could send some of them ahead. That way I wouldn't have to carry as much with me. I cried more than I packed, but at least I was being somewhat productive. I listened to the Quiet Storm show on the radio while asking God for forgiveness and trying to figure out what to do. We could get our marriage annulled with no hard feelings, right? We didn't consummate our marriage any way. Now I'm really tripping. I'm sounding like my uncle; that's what he told me to do once he found out I was married. I can't justify not wanting to be married all of a sudden. What would I base it on? I committed to the relationship and I do love him. I just don't want to hurt anyone. But no matter what I decide, someone is going to end up hurt, and that's serious.

I'm a little backwards in my thinking since I've been a wife for over four months now. Why do I make everything so hard? If I would have just listened, these tears would be tears of joy. But no, I thought I knew and could handle everything, so I deserve whatever I get. This self-loathing session went on for hours until I was interrupted by the telephone. I snatched it up because it's late and I don't want it to wake anyone. As soon as I heard Lamont's voice I felt relieved. All he said was that he made it home, but I was just content that he called. Instantly I was exhausted and laid across the bed on top of clothes and all, and slept until morning.

I jumped up because it was 7:30am and the moving company was going to be here any minute. I threw the rest of the clothes into my chest and started on a box. I never realized I had so much stuff. I had finished just as the truck arrived. I sat in silence as they loaded all of my things. I had reached the point of no return. I signed off on the paperwork and thanked the men for being so careful with my things. Once I shut the door I just stared at the space where my furniture had taken up residence for the weekend. I couldn't believe that it was actually happening. It was almost time for me to go. There was a somber spirit in the house for the rest of the day. The countdown was beginning to take its toll on my family, especially my mom. I think her eyes were about swollen shut from all the crying. I had questioned my decisions for the last time. It was crunch time and I was all in.

The phone rang constantly with friends and family getting the details on my leaving and asking when was the going away party. I couldn't wait to see all of my loved ones gathered together for the last time for who knows how long. Time was really ticking away. I was getting more and more excited, finally embracing the fact that I was a wife and I was getting a chance to travel to some places that other people could only dream of. And I would be with a man that I've loved for years and we were going to share this beautiful experience.

My mom told me of stories of my early childhood when we were stationed in Germany and all the fun and drama that she and my daddy used to have. She said that she prayed that Joseph and I would have a wonderful and lasting marriage. She also filled me in on some tricks of the game. I smiled as I listened while thinking if we could be half as happy as my parents are then I would be okay. I told her of my five-year plan and how I thought things were going to work out. She just smiled and rubbed my back, probably thinking "bless her heart" as she listened to how I had it all figured out. We were going to do this and this and what I was going to allow and what I was not going to stand for. I had it all worked out in my head. I wish my daddy would talk to me like this. I needed his input too but he wasn't ready. Our together time was running out fast. The clock was definitely ticking.

It's party time...

This is my last weekend. I'm so nervous, yet excited. I am on my way to get my hair done for the last time before leaving and I'm trying to get myself together. I can't believe five months went by like that, seems like I just dropped Joseph off at the Atlanta airport. I laughed and cried as I thought about all the stuff I had done in that time. I got to hit Freaknik for the last time; I met R Kelly and hung out in his entourage in ATL for a week, living like a superstar. I got to go to NBA player, Larry Johnson's wedding reception and not only see him, but I met a lot of the NBA's best players and got to party with them.

I hung out hard with The Foundation. We were together all the time. I was really going to miss my girls. Now it was time to leave it all and go start a new chapter in my life. I walked in the salon with a tear-stained face and everyone wanted to know what was bothering me. I explained that I was going to miss everyone and I was just thinking of how good my life is, how great all the people in my world are and how much everyone meant to me. I hugged Kena, my hairdresser, and sat in the chair.

"Give me the hairstyle of the year," I said. "I want to be too cute for my going away party. You're coming aren't you?"

"I'm going to try and make it. You know I'm usually busy on Sundays with church and the family, but I can definitely give you that hairstyle you're looking for." She laid me back and began to wash my hair. As I laid there with my eyes closed Lamont popped into my head. I had avoided telling him for all of these months and now it was time for me to leave and there was no way to get around it. I started crying again but I couldn't even fool myself about this sea of tears. I was absolutely terrified of how he was going to respond when I told him who I really was. Kena just hugged me and handed me some tissue.

"It's going to be alright, girl. God is going to take care of you." She smiled with such confidence. How could she be so sure? I mean, we are very young and marriage is hard work.

"I just hope that I can be a good wife and we are happy. You know what I mean," I mumbled as she led me to the dryer. She patted my hand, gave me a wink and assured me that it was going to be fine. This was a rare day for me. I was going to have most of it to myself. I'd had someone with me at all times for the past five months and my dryer time was my weekly mental escape from all the hustle and bustle that had become my life.

I was in and out of the salon in less than two hours and I really loved my hair. I got at least ten compliments before I even walked out the door. At least I was going to arrive in Germany in style because there was no telling how long it was going to be before I got another real hairdo. I already had my outfit ready for Sunday, this cute little number that I had picked up when I was in Atlanta. I had a few stops to make, picking up gifts and saying my good-byes to people who weren't going to be able to make it to my party. I got a little emotional with each good-bye but at least I got to see them before I left. I didn't open the gifts. I said I would wait until I got to Germany and Joseph and I could open them together. I had to go pick up some things for the party since my mom was at work. I did my running around and got home before the 5 o'clock traffic hit. I hated sitting in traffic so I made it a point to be done or at a sitting point by 4:45.

I had about ten messages on the answering machine. I had zoned out and was staring into space when my daddy walked in the door. We hadn't really talked much over the past couple of months. He asked me if I had all of my documents ready and which airport did I need to be at on Tuesday. Once I answered him he turned around and went upstairs.

That was the hardest part for me. My daddy acted like he hated me at times. I knew he was disappointed in the way that I did it but I didn't think he was going to just shut me out like I didn't exist. When my mom walked in she asked what was the matter and when I told her how I felt, she told me that my daddy didn't hate me and that he was just hurt and didn't want me to leave. That made me feel a little better but I wish he had told me instead of just shutting me out. As soon as that thought entered my head it made me realize that was the same thing I was doing to Lamont. Communication is essential in any type of relationship be it parent to child, husband to wife, or friend to friend. Lesson learned.

The entire weekend was a party. There was nothing that I didn't do. I saw friends and family that I hadn't seen in ages and it made me feel good that I had impacted so many people's lives. I was still inviting people to my party. I had already lost count of how many were coming but I was thinking the more the merrier. The Foundation partied and laughed like there was no tomorrow. In a sense, I guess we were running out of tomorrows, but it wasn't time to be sad now. We still had some memories to make.

Sunday was here before I knew it and even at church I was handing out invites. I wanted any and everybody to celebrate with me. As soon as we got home it was time to transform our house into "Party Central." My family had covered every angle; we had the food, the drinks, balloons and banners. We had it all. There were people everywhere you looked. Cars were parallel parked all the way to the entrance of our neighborhood and we had taken over the clubhouse parking lot. I couldn't have imagined it any better than it was right now. I hugged and kissed so many people that I had at least four different shades of lipstick on my face. There was no age limit, no racial barriers. Just one big party. The DJ had a little something for everyone and he kept the party going.

I was hitting the Butterfly on the dance floor when my cousin handed me the phone. She couldn't make out who it was because of all the commotion. I walked into the hallway bathroom and shut the door.

"Hello," I said assuming it was someone needing directions. Never in a million years was I ready to hear Lamont on the other end.

"What are you doing? Are you having a party or something?" I couldn't breathe. He was supposed to be in Virginia Beach. What was he doing calling me? I just leaned up against the wall with my eyes closed.

"Yeah, we are having a party. How's the beach?" Somehow I managed to speak.

"Oh, it was nice" he replied.

What did he mean 'was?' Why is he speaking in the past tense?

"So I assume you are going to be home?" he said. "I'm at the store and I thought I would swing by and see you." I damn near dropped the phone. What is he doing home? I was feeling light headed like I was going to pass out or something. I managed to get the words "OK" out of my mouth before I collapsed onto the sink.

I sat there for about five minutes before Taz knocked on the door trying to see who was locked up in the bathroom. I managed to get my arm up to the knob and turn it. When I opened it I must have looked like a complete mess because the Foundation pulled me out of the bathroom and sat me on the steps.

"What's wrong with you? Who was that on the phone?" (The Foundation was known for thinking we were bad and could handle any situation).

"Lamont is on his way here," I mumbled. Now we're all sitting on the stairs looking like zombies. How did this happen? This wasn't like I had planned it by no means!

"What are we going to do," they asked. At least they were going to be there with me for support. Their comments made me feel a little better. I looked up and a big sign reading "Best Wishes" was staring me in the face.

"The signs, I need to pull all of the banners down" I said in a panic.

"Give it up, D. You have to tell him," they pleaded. It didn't matter now anyway. He was standing in the doorway looking dazed like a deer caught in headlights. My heart stopped and I didn't want to take my next breath. He wouldn't hurt an unconscious woman. If I could just pass out right now that would be fine. His face was shattered. He couldn't mask his pain or confusion and to make matters worse, he had Brandon and another guy with him. I felt terrible. I was shaking and couldn't get any feeling in my legs to even stand. It was like the music stopped and all I could hear was my heart pounding. I was sweating profusely and became very jittery. I couldn't even swallow. I just sat there and looked at him. My daddy saw what was going on and called him to the kitchen.

"Girl, I'm glad I'm not you. What are you going to do?" my sister asked. My girls nodded in unison. How did it go from "we" to "me" in a matter of minutes? All I could say was "I don't know," as I rested my head in my hands. They all laid their hands on my back and just rubbed on me to try and calm me down. Once I got my breathing together, I tried to stand but my legs gave out, so we all sat back down. My mind was racing. How was I going to say what I had been trying to say for months? It didn't matter now. The signs and gifts and party were painting the ugly truth. I had shut my friend out of one of the most important things that he deserved to know.

Lamont hit that corner in a flash, picked me up and carried me outside. Do you think the Foundation said a blame word? No! They just looked at me, their eyes bulging with pity and sympathy. I was thankful that he picked me up though because my legs still weren't working. But I hate that he carried my out in front of all of these people. Now they are going to think something was wrong. The last thing that I needed was for my male cousins to think he was going to do something to harm me. He was still carrying me and I didn't really know what to expect. Was he going to yell at me and demand that I tell him what was going on? At this point it didn't matter. Whatever he wanted I was going to do. He sat me down on the curb and just stood in front of me with his hands on his side, as I looked at the ground.

"Look at me," he commanded. The rage in his voice made me tremble. I'd never seen him this mad before. I looked up quickly but then looked away. He squatted in front of me and lifted my chin with his finger so that we were eye to eye level. His was a look of sadness and confusion.

"What's going on," he asked. He needed to get an understanding of the big celebration.

"I'm leaving" was all I could manage to say.

"Leaving? Going where?" he asked, still not understanding.

"Away and I don't know when I'll be back. I need for you to go on with your life. Please don't wait for me. You deserve to be happy, too." I rambled in one long breath and again I looked away. He turned my head towards him again and looked me in the eye and said, "I can't let you do this I'm in love with you." My mind started reeling. If he had said those words five months earlier my world would have been a lot less complicated. But tonight it only added sorrow.

"No you don't." That was all I could get out before he placed his finger over my lips.

"Yes, I do. And if you are honest with yourself you are in love with me, too." A tear rolled down his face. Headlights caught my attention before I could reply. Someone was heading right towards us. The car slowed to a stop and the window started to lower. "Hey, Baby I was looking for you. You know I couldn't let you leave without me saying bye."

Great! You have got to be kidding me. I really didn't need this right now. It was Jason, the only other man with whom I'd had a serious, but volatile, relationship. The only man that Lamont couldn't stand more than Joseph was right in front of us. And I'm not strong enough to pull him off if he decides to strike.

I tried to create a diversion. "Hey Jason, I didn't know you were here. When did you get home?"

"I came home today. You know I couldn't let you leave without seeing you." Now he's rubbing it in because he knew Lamont didn't know that I was leaving.

"That's enough," I yelled and a smirk covered his face.

"What's he crying for? If anyone should be crying it should be me," Jason said. He was really working on some physical harm.

"Please stop. Not tonight Jason" I pleaded.

"D." I heard my mom's voice out of the darkness. "Thank you, Lord" I sighed.

"Someone is looking for you at the house. What's going on down here?" My mom said as she surveyed the situation.

"Hey, Ma," Jason said. He was still trying to pull rank. Why won't he just leave, I thought.

"What are you doing down here?" My mom said. She was bothered with this triangle and was ready to break it up. She sent Jason up the hill and told him to park at the clubhouse parking lot. She told Lamont to come with her. I walked away to go see who was looking for me. I looked back at my mom and Lamont and was so thankful that God sent her there when He did. That wouldn't have been positive at all. I was greeted with hugs and well wishes when I made it back to the house. After I had spent some time with my guests the Foundation pulled me upstairs.

"Well, what happened?" They had gathered around waiting for my report.

"Since you all had my back you should already know" I was still a little agitated that they didn't try and help me.

"Girl, he was so upset and that's a whole lot of man to try and calm down." They gave a nervous chuckle. "You know what I'm saying."

"You act like I don't know that. And to make matters worse, guess who pulled up when we were talking, Jason."

"What was he doing down there?" My girls were getting mad.

"Nothing, girl. I wasn't even thinking about him. I was still stunned that Lamont told me he was in love with me." I said it without even thinking.

"What?" they all screamed. "He said what? That's some movie mess right there."

"Who you telling and he was crying, too. I feel like a true villain right now."

"Crying? Girl that's major. He's really in love with you D." The room grew silent. I had really done it this time. My mom knocked on the door and made me come downstairs. Lamont, Brandon and my parents were standing in the kitchen

"Did you know he was our cousin?" My mom said excitedly, pointing at Brandon "Close cousin at that," my uncle chimed in.

"That's good," I said. I was looking at Lamont, and still trying to process what he had just said and still feeling bad for him finding out like this.

He managed to hang around for about 30 more minutes and then he was ready to go. I walked him to the car and told him that I still planned on coming to see him for his birthday, if he wanted to see me.

"Of course I still want to see you," he said as he pulled me into him and kissed me. Not just any kiss. But it was one of those consuming, earth-stopping, breath-taking kisses that exuded all of your emotions. It seemed to last forever. For that moment I had no worries, concerns or regrets. I felt free as if we were floating. It was like our souls were communicating, and we were in sync once again.

When he pulled away my lips were in shock, but they still managed to allow "I love you" to seep through. With everything I had inside of me I loved him, but I knew that I had to let him go.

I walked in the house in a daze. The Foundation was ready to bring me back to life. They couldn't control the sadness that I was feeling, but they could help me forget about it for a little while. They walked over to me and gave me a group hug, wiped away my tears and proceeded to dance around me, trying to lighten my mood. The Percolator came on and my smile emerged. My hands went up and I was in the middle of the living room getting my party on. We danced until the wee hours of the morning. Exhausted, we were all sitting around the wall and spread out in the floor. The majority of the guest had long left. This had become the after party with about twenty of us remaining. We sat around and laughed and talked, not really wanting this night to end. We knew that in less than 48 hours I would be leaving and that was too final right now. We finally called it a night, put the house back together and everyone went home. This was the perfect temporary fix, but tomorrow was inevitable.

Hard to say good-bye...

A power nap would have to suffice. I needed to be out of the house by 7:00 am. I had to hit the road so that I could be in Greensboro when Lamont woke up. I took my shower, got dressed and went out to start my car. I put the key in the ignition, pushed in my clutch and turned the key, but nothing happened. I looked at my dashboard and tried it again- Nothing. How could this be? I just had this car serviced from top to bottom two days ago. What was going on now? I tried one more time still nothing. I looked at my watch and time was ticking I went back in the house and woke my daddy up so he could check my car out. He asked me where I was going this time of morning, and when I told him, he wanted to know why. I told him that it was Lamont's birthday and I promised him that I would spend it with him. My daddy didn't say much. He just slipped on his jeans and went outside. It didn't make a difference though. He couldn't get it started either. How in the world could this be happening today? I reluctantly dialed Lamont's number and when he answered I explained what was going on.

"You are not going to believe this, but my car won't start."

"What do you mean it won't start?" he interrupted.

"Just what I said. I tried it three times and I even got my daddy to try it. I can't explain it after I spent all of that money to make sure it was in excellent condition. I'm sorry, but I'm not going to be able to come up there today." Lamont paused, and then offered to come and get me. I told him that would be too much. Most of our time would be spent driving. I told him that I would leave his gift with my mom and he could come and get it when he came back home. That wasn't what he wanted to hear, but really nothing that I was going to say that day was going to be pleasing to him. If I knew that I was going to have to tell him on the phone I would have told him a long time ago.

"I can't believe that I'm not going to get to see you today, but after that kiss last night it's probably for the best." I said. Lamont was racking his brain trying to figure out how he could see me today and told me that he would call me back in a little while. In the meantime, I went back to sleep or at least that's what I'll call it for lack of a better word. I tossed and turned more than anything. I really wanted to sit down and get everything out in the open. I needed to explain why I did what I did and let him know that I do love him, but I want him to move on and have a wonderful life. I knew that he wouldn't feel like that initially, but with time it would come. But all of that was out the window now. The most I could do was listen to him on the phone.

All of the thinking was wearing me out. My eyes were closed but there was no rest. I finally gave up and rolled out of bed. I woke Taz and told her to get ready so we could strike out for the good-bye tour. There were a few people that I wanted to see one last time. We were headed out the door when Lamont called to see if I had come up with a plan. I told him that it just wasn't going to happen and he lost it. I just listened as he ranted on the phone. I couldn't blame him. I had just pulled the rug from under him. For him to even talk to me was good enough for me. He asked me to listen to something so I sat on the arm of the sofa and put the TV on mute. Blackstreet's "Before I Let You Go" was blaring in the background. I listened to the words until my emotions got the best of me. I told him that I had to go and I would call him later. I told him Happy Birthday as we got off the phone. How could I be so insensitive? Of course, this isn't a happy birthday and it was my fault.

We pulled out of the driveway and as I crossed over I-85 North the thought of hitting the highway did cross my mind. But then all I could think was everything happens for a reason so I'm going to go where I said I was going to say good-bye to my family. I stopped at my grandparents first. Granny Fannie dropped some words of wisdom in my spirit and prayed for me. I hugged and kissed my grandparents and headed to my aunt's house. This was turning out to be one of the most depressing days of my life. I was saying good-bye to everyone and everything that I've always known and loved. All of the tears were beginning to take an effect on me. We pulled into my aunt's driveway and I sat there for a minute before we got out of the car and walked inside. My cousin Kira was already crying. This was not good. We hugged non-stop for a while before I pulled away and told her that I had to go because I still had a lot of people to see. When we turned to walk away my aunt hugged me and told me she loved me and then held Kira as we pulled off.

Taz was silent for a little while but then she asked if I was alright. I said 'yes' but we still had to go see Rochelle, or "Wanda" as we like to call her because she could cry you a river at the drop of a hat. She met us in the parking lot. I took a deep breath and got out of the car. Her eyes were already swollen from crying and she wasn't ready to stop. She asked me not to go and I almost considered it. I never thought that my leaving would cause my loved ones so much pain. Just then her phone rang and she told me it was for me.

"He's called here three times already," she said as she handed me the phone

"Who is it?" I whispered while putting the phone to my ear. I could hear Blackstreet in the background and I knew it was Lamont.

"Hello" I said curiously. It was Lamont's voice on the other end. He asked me what time I was going home and Rochelle went off.

"She's telling her family good-bye. If we can handle it then I know you can. She's going through enough. She doesn't need you making her feel worse." I covered the phone and begged her to hush. She got up and walked into the kitchen. I talked to him for a brief moment more and then I had to get back down the road. I still had a bunch of people that I wanted to see.

"I'll call you when I get home, okay?"

He sighed and said "Okay."

I hugged Rochelle once more and her boyfriend had to pry us apart. She had been more than a cousin. We were like sisters. I could feel the sea of tears coming. I didn't want to have an outburst in front of them, so I jumped in the car and pulled off throwing my hand out the window, as we exited the parking lot.

Taz and I drove without speaking, listening to the radio and looking straight ahead. We made a few more stops before heading home. I got to see a couple of aunts and cousins before it was time to go. I was getting tired, and we had been gone all day long. When we finally pulled in our driveway my mom was waiting on us. We had been gone since this morning and it was almost dusk. She wanted to spend some time with me on my last day. So I spent the remainder of the evening with my parents and my sister. We didn't say much, but being together was more than enough.

The phone rang off the hook. One after the other people called to tell me goodbye. One of the last calls was Lamont. We talked, well really we just held the phone, for about 30 minutes and I told him that I would call him back after I got out of the shower. The phone rang while I was hanging up the receiver and it was Jason. He wanted to come by and see me since he hadn't had a chance to spend any time with me. I looked at the clock and I told him that I only had a little time but he could stop by. I sat my bags by the door and slipped on my shoes. He came in and spoke to everyone before we walked outside to talk. His pager went off and it was his brother. He needed Jason to pick him up. Jason asked if I would ride with him. I told him that would be fine as long as we weren't gone long. I told my parents that I would be back and we pulled off.

We rode and talked, and for the first time today I laughed. Jason and I use to have a relationship. Even though we didn't work out we were still good friends. He told me that he wanted me to be happy. He asked me to promise that if my marriage wasn't working out and I wanted to leave, that I would come home and not try to make it work just to prove everyone wrong. I promised and we started talking about something else.

"What about Lamont?" He probed.

I got quiet for a minute and then I said, "He's going to be fine." I paused for a moment before continuing, "He told me that he loved me last night. I really wasn't expecting that."

Jason looked over at me before he replied. "Everybody loves you so what is he talking about?" I had a flashback of last night- Lamont's words, that kiss. It was too surreal.

"No, he's in love with me, for real, and I feel awful because it's like

I led him on. I really hate that it turned out like this, but I don't know what else to do."

Jason grabbed my hand and squeezed it before he spoke.

"Listen, if I thought me telling you that I loved you would be enough to make you stay I would have tried it, too. But I know that your heart is with Joseph and I want you to be happy. Don't let last night stand in the way of your happiness. You made your decision; stick with it. And we both know I'm not a Joseph fan, so that's all I'm going to say on that topic. Just be happy."

I checked my watch and the time was flying. We turned into my neighborhood and I got choked up because I knew this was going to be the last time that I came home for a long time. Jason walked me to the door and gave me a big hug as he told me good-bye. I walked in the house and went straight to my room. When I walked pass my window I noticed that he was still sitting in front of the house. I closed my blinds and laid across my bed. The hall light came on, and my Daddy began exercising his parental rights.

"Do you see what time it is? We need to be out of here in an hour. Do you have everything ready?" I smiled because no matter what, I was going to always be my daddy's little girl. I pulled out the cards that I had bought for my parents and my sister and made sure that I placed them in my purse. I jumped in the shower and just stood there for a while. I hummed a song while I washed each body part at least three times. This was it. I was hours away from my new life. I dried myself off and massaged the lotion into my skin and slipped on my clothes. I looked at the clock and then at the phone. Should I call him or just let it go? Before I knew it I was dialing and he was on the other end. "I thought you had forgotten about me," he slurred. I had woke him up. I chuckled and told him he couldn't have thought that. I told him that I was about to leave and I wished him the best. I told him that I would miss him but that we would both be okay. I was getting choked up so I ended our conversation with good-bye. There was no response from the other end.

The drive to the airport in Columbia wasn't long enough. We checked my luggage and went into town to grab something to eat. We ate slowly like that was going to make a difference, but breakfast couldn't last forever. We headed back for the airport and pulled into the parking lot. The four of us sat motionless and quiet. My daddy sighed and opened the door. I followed him out of the car. Taz was next, but my mom wouldn't budge. I didn't say anything to her for a minute because I didn't want to see her cry. But my time was ticking and I wanted her to walk me to my gate. She couldn't do it at first but my daddy talked her out of the car. While they were walking away I headed back to the van and placed their cards in their seats. I prayed that the messages that I wrote inside each card would make my leaving a little better. I closed the door, and put on my jacket and took a deep breath. I was ready to go. It seemed like I barely made it to the gate in time. They called my section and it was time for me to board.

That was the beginning of the end. I had never seen so many tears and they were coming at me from all angles. Taz and my mom were uncontrollable, while my daddy tried to keep his composure. He hugged me and told me that I could always come home, that it was just a phone call away. I grabbed Taz and just held her. I was going to miss my baby sister. For the past 15 years I could count how many days we weren't together. I kissed her and walked over to my mom. To touch her was like being electrocuted, all of her emotions transferred to me as soon as I hugged her. I held on for dear life. It was so hard to let go. I took one more deep breath and then I walked over to the gate door. I looked back and waved one last time.

My family was an emotional wreck, but there was nothing I could do about that at this point. I was sitting in the first row and as I fastened my seatbelt I could still hear my family's sobs. The flight attendant, who had watched as we said our farewells, came to me and asked if I wanted to go and say goodbye one last time. I thought about it and then reconsidered

"No, thank you. It would only make things worse." She pulled the door shut as I leaned my head back and cried. She placed some tissue in my lap as she walked to the back of the plane. I looked back at the airport as we taxied away and I could still see my family looking out the window of the terminal window. I looked down at my wedding ring and prayed to God that I had done the right thing.

New beginnings…

We had a layover in Philly so I figured I would check out the airport. I didn't get very far before I saw a payphone. I had a few coins on me so I decided to kill some time. I called my family first to let them know that I had made it to Philly okay. If I would have had my phone book on me I would have called some of my relatives that I had here in Philly. I called Rochelle and she called Kira and before I knew it the whole Foundation was on the phone trying to have a positive attitude about my leaving. Then I just had to do it. I had to hear Lamont's voice one last time. He picked up on the first ring and I cried like a baby. He tried his best to console me but he ended up crying too. I begged him to forgive me and he told me that he already had. He told me to enjoy myself and to take care of myself. I was staring at the gift shop directly in front of me when I heard my name on the PA system.

"Oh my goodness I have to go they are paging me" I shouted as I rushed him off the phone.

"No. Wait I..." He started to speak but I didn't let him finish.

"I can't. I don't have time the plane is waiting on me. I love you." I slammed the phone down and ran for my gate. The cabin erupted in applause as soon as I stepped on board. The flight attendant said she understood as I apologized repeatedly. She assured me it wasn't a problem and giggled as she said "We weren't going to leave without you."

I sat in my seat too afraid to move again. I didn't even think I was going to take a trip to the restroom while we were in the air.

Of course, that promise didn't last two hours. Before I knew it I was up moving around the cabin. I was becoming restless and still had hours to go. I realized that I never told Joseph my flight number. How was he going to find me? I didn't know how I was going to feel when I saw him. Was I going to rush to him or would I be withdrawn when I got there? With limited options to choose from for entertainment, I drifted off to sleep, hoping the next time I opened my eyes we would be landing. I ended up taking two more power naps before I heard the "fasten your seat belt" announcement. The flight attendant passed out warm face clothes for us to freshen up before we landed. I sat up straight as I stretched my back and my legs and let out a big yawn. I rushed to the restroom and brushed my teeth, touched up my lips and made sure my hair was in place.

I had butterflies in my stomach as we touched down. I gave a quick "Thank you, Lord" praise and waited for the plane to come to a complete stop. I stood up, but couldn't move for a minute afraid of what was going to happen when I walked through that door. I reached up and pulled down my carryon bags and stepped off the plane. There were no screams of joy, bouquets or even hugs and kisses. In fact there was no one there to meet me at all. I walked around the airport alone. I would stop and wait on one side and then walk to the other side. There was still no sign of Joseph anywhere. I had no way of contacting him to see if he was stuck in traffic or what. I was just here.

I knew I had to call my parents. They would start worrying soon. But what was I going to say when they asked me "Where's Joseph?" They really weren't going to accept the truth very well. That he's not here and I don't know where he is. But I didn't want to pretend like he's here and then he calls them looking for me. I finally broke down and called. I figured that if they asked I would tell them. But, if they didn't, I wouldn't say a word. When they answered it was like I hadn't heard their voices in years instead of hours. They asked what I was doing and I said waiting on my luggage. My change didn't last long, since it was an international call, but it was long enough for me to hear them and calm my nerves.

I walked over to the help desk and explained my situation. I told her all I knew was that we lived on California Strassa and I knew Joseph's social security number. She took his information and plugged it into the system to find out what unit he was in. Then she called his sergeant and told him what was going on. The sergeant informed her that there had been a mix up and he was at the wrong airport. Joseph was actually nearby, just around the corner, in fact. The sergeant said he would have him paged and assured her that Joseph would be there shortly. I had already told the customer service agent that if he wasn't there by the time the next plane left for the states that I was going back home and we would chalk this up as a learning experience. She couldn't tell if I was serious or not so she tried to laugh it off. Bless her heart. If only she knew how serious I was.

This was beginning to look like a sign to me. I guess the angels must have been listening because no sooner than I got that sentence out of my mouth Joseph came through the doors with this huge smile on his face. I was glad that someone could find the humor in this because I was all tapped out. He opened his arms as he walked toward me while I was extending my arms while saying "don't even think about it." I had spent my first two hours in Germany alone in an airport not knowing where my husband or my home was. The best thing for him to do was to grab my bags and keep it moving.

He introduced his friend, slash driver, Eric but I wasn't in the mood to mingle. I just wanted to get home, take a shower and lay down. They talked while I observed my new surroundings. Eric was getting on Joseph for not having the proper information and leaving me stranded. Every now and then I would throw in a smart comment or two, but for the most part I was over it now. We pulled up to this drab colored building with one steel door and a bunch of windows. I assumed we were at the barracks not knowing this would be what I would call home for the next three years. We walked in and I just stood there and took it all in- hardwood floors, no central air conditioning, two bedrooms and one bathroom. My first apartment, our first home.

"I can't wait for our furniture to get here" were the first words out of my mouth. I walked into what I assumed was the kitchen. It had to be since I was looking at a refrigerator, but where was the stove? The guys laughed as I asked the inevitable question. Joseph reached over and lifted a lid and behold there was our stove, none like I had ever seen before but a stove none the least. I walked into the bathroom and the tub was so big we could both sit in it with no problem. When I walked into our bedroom I remembered that we still hadn't consummated our marriage yet. We'll have to get right on that. I peeped in the guestroom and then walked back out into the living room. I can't believe I'm really here and we are together. I couldn't wait until I got to this point, but now what?

Eric left while I was taking a hot shower. I came out and put on some sweats. I sat down beside Joseph and laid my head on his lap. He rubbed my back until I fell asleep. When I woke up, I was lying in his arms on the sofa. He kissed my forehead and told me how happy he was that I was home.

"Home" I repeated looking him in his eyes as I gave him a kiss.

We got up and walked towards the bedroom. Joseph checked the door and cut off the TV and lights. Once I reached the bedroom door, I stopped walking.

"What's wrong?" he asked a little confused.

"You do realize that technically this is our wedding night, don't you?"

With a big kool- aid grin he said "Oh yeah" and scooped me up in his arms and carried me over the threshold.

The following day I had to go sign in and get my ID card. I also signed up for the driving class, which was mandatory to get your German driver's license. We didn't have a car so we had to catch a bus over to the Main Post. It was different relying on public transportation to get where I needed to go. My daddy had to get my car checked out and then have it shipped over so that we would have a means of transportation. While we waited for the bus to take us back to our neighborhood, I spotted a telephone and called home. Because of the time difference, I could only reach my grandmother. Everyone else was at work or school. We talked for a few minutes and then she talked to Joseph until the bus pulled up.

What I would wear at home this time of year was not cutting it in Germany. The wind was going through me like a knife. I layered as much as possible but I was still cold. We had to go to the PX to get me some suitable clothing after we left the JAG office. The JAG office is the legal office where you fill out all of your paperwork and get your ID card. Once we got to the PX and the warmth unthawed me, I made a beeline to the hair salon to make an appointment. I couldn't wait until I got familiar with everything so that I wouldn't have to depend on Joseph to be my tour guide. I met a hairstylist named Sonja and scheduled an appointment for Friday. That way I would still be on schedule, just like I was at home. I caught up with Joseph in the shoe department. He had found me some nice shoes that should keep my toes warm and now we were looking for a jacket and some sweaters. We ran into Keith, one of his friends from California, and decided to get together for a card party on Friday. Great I'll get to meet some folks. I decided to grab a couple of books while I was at the PX so that I would have something to keep me busy for the remainder of the week.

We made our way over to the electronics department where I spotted a phone and it dawned on me that we still didn't have a phone at home. I asked when he thought our phone would be on? He went through this long spill about how expensive phone service was in Germany; and how they charge you by clicks and not minutes; and how a guy from his unit's wife had run their bill up calling back to the "world" to listen to the soap operas every day and blah, blah, blah. But by the time he was finished preaching, my question was still "when do you think we will have our phone?"

"I need to have a way to communicate with my family and friends back home. How do you function without a phone? Oh, I forgot you don't, because you can use one at work. I've always had a phone and I'm too old to not have one now." One of the sales associates was all in our conversation and chuckled as I was grabbing different cordless phones and fussing. Then out of nowhere Joseph walks up with the biggest phone in the store. The phone had a built in clock so he could time my conversations. To keep our phone bill down was his excuse.

"Yeah, yeah as long as I have a phone I don't care." I sighed loudly, frowning at the phone.

"I'll call the phone company first thing in the morning," he promised, as he placed the ancient looking phone in the shopping cart.

When we got home I made some hamburger helper and veggies like I had really done something and popped in a movie. Before I knew it, it was 10:00 pm, Joseph's bedtime. I was really having a problem with this early bedtime, but on the other hand I didn't have anything else to do either. I gave in and called it a night as well. Something is going to have to give, I thought to myself. I'm going to drive myself crazy if I don't find a job. Once we were all tucked in the nighttime games began.

5:00 a.m. came like a thief in the night. It seemed as if we had just gone to bed. He was rushing because he had overslept. We were going to have to work on us sleeping together every night and still being able to function in a timely manner. I asked him what he wanted for breakfast. I figured that was the least I could do since I could go back to sleep while he was at work. I got up, whipped up a breakfast sandwich and wrapped it up for him. I sat and watched him get ready with a smile on my face. I was happy to finally be with my husband in peace. After my goodbye kiss, I watched him leave for work. As soon as the door closed it hit me. What in the world was I going to do with myself all day. I unpacked my bags and arranged my clothes in my closet and drawers. I walked outside and took in the crisp air. Once I was back inside I swept the floor and retreated to the sofa. In my five year plan I guess I overlooked the obvious, what in the world was I going to do over here. Being just a housewife had never been on my 'to do' list, but what could I do? I didn't finish college and I was sure the jobs were limited on base, but I was going to have to find something before I went crazy. I found a stash of books in the guestroom. I grabbed one and that was my companion the rest of my day.

Before I knew it, it was 4:00 pm, an hour before Joseph would be home. I should start cooking something. I went into the kitchen and opened the cabinets and frig where I saw a lot of single man meals- ramen noodles, microwave dinners, tuna and stuff like that. It was going to take a miracle to make a meal out of that. I finally found something. Fish sticks, instant potatoes, peas and cornbread. That would have to do today. I had it all done, as well as my hair, when Joseph walked in the house. I was pretty proud of myself. He had something to eat as soon as he walked through the door. I met him at the door with a hug and a kiss and so much appreciation to have someone to talk to that it was a little overwhelming for him. I asked him ten questions back to back, almost in a single breath. I didn't have any friends and I didn't have a phone, so I treasured my talk time.

After dinner Joseph took a shower and probably needed a break from me while I cleaned up the kitchen. When we were finished we relaxed on the sofa. He was playing his game and I was finishing my book. I could do this part every day. It was cozy, yet he was doing his thing and I was doing mine. He gave in before I did. At around 9:30 he started shutting down.

"You have got to be kidding me," I grumbled feeling like a child. "I haven't gone to bed this early in over ten years. What is going on?"

"This is what time I go to bed during the week," he replied.

I must add this to the list of things that we are learning about each other. I never thought to ask something like "What time do you like to go to bed at night?" We definitely should have taken a pre-marital counseling class for this one.

"So what am I supposed to do," I quizzed.

"You either lay down with me or you stay up. It doesn't matter, but I have to get my sleep. I have a lot to do during the day." He shrugged his shoulders as he stood up. I couldn't believe it, but when he cut his game off, I marked my page and walked to the room, too. I don't really know why because I wasn't sleepy by any means. So I waited until I heard him snoring and I made my way back to the living room. I picked up my new best friend and continued with my reading. Between 11pm and 3am I finished my book and stumbled back to the bed. I laid down as softly as I could, rolled onto my stomach, pulled the covers over my head and I was out.

I felt Joseph's kiss on my forehead. I nodded my head, but I didn't open my eyes. I figured I would just sleep as long as I could and then go from there. I got up around 11am and washed my face, brushed my teeth and plopped down on the sofa. What was I going to do today? I still needed to get familiar with my surroundings, but my exploring was limited due to a lack of a vehicle. I figured that I would just walk to the PX and kill some time. I got up, took a nice long shower and got dressed. I could do everything in slow motion since I had nothing but unclaimed hours ahead of me. I glanced over at the phone for some wishful thinking and mentally admitted that on a day like today I know that would be trouble. I grabbed my jacket and headed out on my new adventure.

I took in nature's beauty and greeted the many people that I passed. I took long deep breaths and concentrated on planning my new life. I would have a Lamont flashback every now and then, just concerned with how he was doing. I was proud that I hadn't snuck away to a payphone to call him or asked about him on the sly to my family. I knew that once I was gone it would get better. I tried to tell everyone that once Joseph and I were finally together everything would be just fine.

I arrived at my new babysitter, the PX, in no time. I knew I could waste hours just walking around looking at stuff. I purposely left my ATM card so that I wouldn't be tempted to waste money. I spent at least an hour looking at CDs. I've always loved music and was amazed at all the new releases that they had. I had figured there would be lag time in them arriving over here.

As I was leaving the electronics department I could have sworn I saw Lamont. Now I know it was just my mind playing tricks on me, but it seemed so real. I shook it off and continued to walk on. Then I could hear his voice and I knew I was hallucinating. Could I miss him that badly? Perhaps I could send him a card. I walked over to the card section and grabbed a couple of those cards that express exactly what you are feeling inside just to keep me sane. Of course, the first line of the card said more than I would ever want to admit, that I really loved him and wished we had an opportunity to work on us. And how if I would have waited on God that none of this would be happening. Deciding against that one I put it back and read the next one that mentioned how fortunate I was to have a friend like him. Now that one would work. I read a few more before I put them all back and walked over to the jewelry department. I really wanted a new ring.

I accepted my diamond dust when I was in California, but it didn't look like any of the engagement rings that we had looked at before. I found out while I was in Cali that his boy Gary had convinced him not to spend that much money. He told him that if I really loved him, I would accept it. He followed his advice, and of course, I accepted it because I was so in love. But in my mind I was thinking what in the world am I going to tell my family since I had already set the standard for what I wasn't going to accept? Another "never say what you won't do" moment. I found some really nice rings a little pricey, but still nice. I looked at some watches and when I focused on the time I realized that I had spent way more time in the PX than I had planned.

As I was heading out of the store Joseph was coming in. We both smiled as we walked to each other, hugged and kissed. I asked him how his day went and what was he doing at the PX? He said that when he got home and I wasn't there he knew this was the only place that I could have been. I told him that I was on my way home to cook one of my gourmet meals and we both started laughing. He decided that we would eat out tonight and I didn't have a problem with that.

This became one of our traditions. Thursdays would forever be our Date Night.

We laughed the entire time we were at Popeye's and people would look at our table and smile. We couldn't figure out if it was because we looked like two teenagers sitting over there or because we enjoyed each other so much? It really didn't matter what they were thinking. We were loving life. Joseph told me that we were going to rent a car for the weekend and go sightseeing. *Now we're talking.* I had something to look forward to. It was getting late and cold so we headed back to the house, but not before stopping by the video store to get a movie for tonight. We raced each other to see who would make it home first doing more laughing than running. We got home and took our showers and popped in the movie. We made a compromise; since he went to bed so early we agreed to sleep on the futon in the living room. We laid on the futon and watched until we drifted off to sleep. There was no complaining from me tonight. I think I went to sleep first.

It was morning and I popped out of bed excited because I had somewhere to go today. I fixed Joseph's breakfast and cut on the TV while he was getting ready. I went back to sleep once he left. I didn't sleep long. I was too excited about getting my hair done and going somewhere this weekend. You couldn't tell me anything. I got dressed and walked down to the hair salon.

Sonja was just finishing her client as I signed in. She was cool and I knew right then that she was the one. She was going to be in charge of my hair for the next three years. I sat there at least an hour after she finished with my hair. It wasn't like I had a list of things to do to occupy my time. Once I left the salon I went to return the movie and stopped by the PX. I saw a job posting and figured if I was going to be here every day I might as well get paid for it. I picked up an application to fill out later. I made a quick lap around the store and headed home.

I began filling out my application and then started reading over the schedules and responsibilities. I didn't know if I would like working weekends or nights, but I had to do something. I have worked since I was 18. Not only was I used to my own money, there would be more for us to do things with. I also needed to have some interactions with people instead of being cooped up in the house all day. Once I finished, I laid on the futon and read a few chapters in my book before I took a nap. I slept cute of course, on my stomach with my chin resting on my hands propped up on two pillows, because I wanted Joseph to see my hair and I wasn't sure how it would hold up once I went to sleep.

The blaring sound of my alarm clock startled me as I rolled over in my own bed. I had been dreaming of yesteryear the whole time. I was dreaming of a time when my life was simple and fun. Yet it had seemed like the here and now. I finally got my bearings and realized that I had overslept. My alarm had been ringing for over 30 minutes. I bolted out of the bed and ran through the shower. Thankfully I was pleased with the first outfit that I pulled from the closet. I can't believe I had overslept. How in the world did that happen? I pulled myself together and headed for the door. I had to rush back and grab the divorce papers from my night stand. I started the car, ran and placed the papers in the mailbox and raised the flag to alert the carrier. No sooner had I done that did I reconsider, reach in and remove them. As I shook my head I reasoned with myself, confessing that I needed a little more time.

On the drive to work I kicked it into high gear once I hit I-85. My job had been my only true solace throughout this whole divorce ordeal. I was reminiscing about the morning after Joseph told me that he needed some space. I remember getting up like it was any other day and dressed for work. I wore this nice camel colored suit and some black pumps and a nice scarf to tie it all together. I walked into work with my best smile and went straight into my office and shut the door. I fell up against the wall and slid to the floor. It was safe to cry in here. This was my safety zone. No one would bother me. They won't even notice the difference. That's the lie I told myself. That lasted all of ten minutes.

The next thing I knew I was in the Human Resources office with a phone pointed in my face and a hotline number written on a sticky note. I pleaded my case trying to prove that I was going to be fine. How ironic that they knew more than my family because I didn't know how to utter the words "I'm getting a divorce". It was never in my plans and I was really confused as to what I should do next. For the past 12 years

I had lived, ate and slept our life together and now it was all a figment of my imagination. I was finding it hard to breathe all of a sudden and now the entire room was flooding with tears.

That's exactly why I didn't want to tell anyone. I can't handle that look of pity. That "oh, bless her heart" look makes me want to scream. I paused as the counselor answered the phone. What was I supposed to say? I don't need a therapist. I'm a strong independent woman that can make it on my own. I don't need a shrink or a damn black couch to keep me focused. The next thing I remember I was agreeing to meet with a doctor that afternoon. Wow how time flies!

My new reality...

I rushed to the time clock. I don't know why. I was already late. I slipped into my office and as soon as I got comfortable the three amigos were at my door. "Well did you call him and give him a piece of your mind?" Liz asked, her hand on her hip. I swear that girl was a sista in another life.

"No, I didn't. But I did speak to him. He asked if I was alright. I didn't have a response for that since I was officially ending the only life I knew."

"What does he mean are you alright? He's got some nerve!" Janice interrupted already crying. She's so sensitive. I think she's cried the most out of all of us. Carla didn't say anything really. She was more concerned with whether I was really dealing with my feelings. I assured her that I was. I told them that I had a lot to get done in a little bit of time because I had to meet with Dr. Higgins today. I didn't know how long I would be gone. The next three hours flew by and before I knew it I had to leave. I clocked out and headed for my session.

"Lyfetime" by Eryka Badu came on the car radio and it was all bad after that. I don't know when the first tear fell, but it must have been a while ago because my eyes were red, my cheeks stained, and my shirt wet. I tried to get myself together in the parking lot, but it was useless. I gave up and threw on some dark shades to cover the Stop signs I was calling eyes.

The receptionist knew it was one of those days and tried to bring a smile to my face. But although I wanted to smile, something inside would not allow it today. I grabbed the latest magazine and waited patiently for my turn. Thank goodness the waiting room was empty. I hated being that woman that couldn't control her emotions, especially in front of people. After about five minutes, Dr. Higgins called me into his office. I don't know if the receptionist had warned him or what, but today he had a cup of hot tea ready for me. I sat in front of the mug and reached inside my purse. I slammed the divorce papers on the table and stared out the window. I didn't know what else to do. It was actually time to take my next step.

Dr. Higgins was going to need three note pads for our session today. He was really a treasure. He allowed me to express all the feelings, whether good or bad. And he didn't try and fix it. He just listened. He was a husband, father and pastor as well. I had grown really comfortable with him and now we developed a valuable relationship. We discovered that I had gone to school with his youngest daughter. Small world. Here I could speak my mind without fear of retribution.

My family and friends meant well, but they hated to see me in such pain. Every tear only enraged them more and more, and knowing that, I hid a lot of pain in the beginning. I found comfort in writing and that was my way of expressing what was going on inside my heart and mind. I remember in our first session Dr. Higgins did most of the talking. I was amazed at how much he knew about me without even knowing me. One statement that he made while talking was so profound. He said when couples are on the verge of breaking up they usually do one of two things- have a baby or buy a house. Then he looked me in the eye and asked which one I got. "The house," I mumbled.

Dr. Higgins picked up the divorce papers, studied them for a moment, and placed them back on the table. He cleared his throat and told me, "I know it doesn't seem like it now, but it's going to get better. It just takes time. Are you alright?" I couldn't speak yet so I took a few long deep breaths. I truly didn't know what I was feeling. I was numb, but that's about all I could describe at this moment. The fountain in his office was really soothing and I was able to relax a little. I just started to talk.

"You know, this wasn't his first affair and for all I know this could be the same woman. I received a phone call three years ago, while we were living in Fayetteville. I listened as a woman told me that she didn't know we were still together. I gave her a pardon because he really could have told her that. I called him on three-way and accomplished absolutely nothing. I sat back as they argued back and forth until the sound of their voices made me sick and I took over the conversation. I explained to the woman that she didn't have the power to break us up. Only he and I could do that, because we were the only ones that made that covenant of marriage with God. I let her know that I wasn't upset with her but if it happened again then I would deal with her, too. I said 'thank you' and hung up the phone. Now as for him, I had one of two choices- either I hurt him or I leave. And right then it was safer for me to leave. I called my in-laws, because I couldn't call my parents. Just in case I forgave him they may not be as understanding. I told his parents what had happened. Then I made a guest appearance at his job and left town. We still laugh about how fast I made it home that day. We lived two and a half hours away and my brother-in-law claims that I made it home in less than 30 minutes."

I chuckled and Dr. Higgins questioned what was so funny. I told him that people always asked me if I saw the signs and I would say 'no.' I didn't see them because I wasn't looking for them. In hindsight, there were flags all over the place- the extra practices, the attitudes, mood swings and acting withdrawn. And I can't forget the beautiful two carat, princess cut "you deserve it" diamond ring. I stopped talking and just shook my head, what's that old passage by Seneca? "Eyes will not see when the heart wishes them to be blind." Now I see.

"You never finished telling me about Germany. Do you keep in touch with your friends from over there?" Doc asked.

"Are you serious? I talk to at least one of them almost every night. You know when I lost all that weight and couldn't sleep they would check on me and help keep my spirits up. We would talk about how God will never put more on you than you can bear and they would tell me that I was an inspiration to them. My determination and will encouraged them. This was funny to me because there were so many nights that I would bargain with God and just wanted to give up. I have said on more than one occasion that if I didn't wake up in the morning that would be fine with me. But that was not God's plan, so here I sit today. You know what haunts me now though is "what if." What if I would have chosen Lamont instead? Would I be here or would I be a happy wife with my husband, house, 2.5 children and a dog like the statistics suggest? I know I can't live in the past but, it's so much easier than moving forward. Do you realize that I'm almost 30 and I don't know how to date? I never thought I would have a need to. Lamont was the sweetest, most understanding God-fearing man and he loved me with all his heart. But what sticks out in my mind the most is that he loved me unconditionally, and you just don't find that. You know what I mean? Of course parents display this type of love, but this was a man that gave all of himself to me. My leaving hurt him deeply, but when I came back he forgave me."

"Are you ready to talk about him today?" Dr. Higgins asked. He had tricked me. The room was suddenly stifled.

"No… not yet", I reluctantly answered.

"You know that you are going to have to deal with it one day and the sooner you deal with it and let it go the better it will be for you," Dr. Higgins said with a raised eyebrow.

I got up and walked towards the window. I gazed out as if I was looking at a large teleprompter and my lines were running across the screen.

"Divorce is like death but the pain doesn't end for you. Life as you know it is over and no matter how much you miss your old life, you can't go back. You go from being a person to being a zombie. You live in a shell that you are sometimes afraid to come out of but you don't have a choice. I wish I could redo a lot of things, especially the first year that we were separated. I was so angry with God, life, men everything that I acted out instead of being faithful and allowing God to do what He was going to do. I just couldn't understand how I did all that I was supposed to do and I still lost in the end. And I didn't just lose my husband and my house I lost me for a while." I exhaled and started again.

"I didn't have any regards for people, time or life for that matter. I was out of control. I played the game with the best of them. I had successfully detached myself emotionally from dating. I had lost respect for relationships. I had given up on love. My motto was now "get him before he gets me." Instead of church functions and missionary meetings I concentrated on planning my next motorcycle excursion. Motorcycles were my new love. Street races had taken the place of dating and I was surprisingly relaxed in that environment. Instead of making sure I had on something cute, I made sure I had on something comfy just in case I had to run. Making a mad dash from the police came with the territory. That was the exact opposite of me and I think that's what really drew me to that scene. No one knew me so I could reinvent myself. I'd always loved motorcycles, but Joseph felt they were too dangerous so I didn't get one. But now he's gone, so that's my next goal. I'm going to buy my very own bike," I stated proudly.

"So you're rebelling now?" the doctor said jokingly trying to lighten my mood still waiting on that patented smile that he loved to call 'Sunshine.' But I just wasn't feeling that smile today.

"I was getting what I wanted and didn't have to answer to anyone about it, that's all," I said in a harsh tone. I quickly apologized. I wasn't mad at him. I was just frustrated with my life and was ready for this part to be over. I walked back over and sat down.

"Can you have your secretary drop these in the mail for me, please? I don't think that I can do it on my own," I said. I slid the divorce papers over toward him.

"Sure, that's not a problem at all. They will go out in our afternoon mail run," he said calmly.

"Thank you so much. I'll call and let him know that they are in the mail and to have a nice life," I said sarcastically.

"Maybe you shouldn't call him just yet. Maybe you should give him some time because, believe it or not, he's hurting too." Dr. Higgins suggested.

"Hurting for what? He created this mess. He should be ecstatic," I grunted. Then I affirmed my future.

"You know what, enough about him. From now on it's about me. I just want to be what, where and with whom God wants me to be. I can't worry about the past relationships. I'll just have to take the good with the bad, count it as a learning experience and move on." I threw my hands in the air.

"Now that sounds like a text book answer if I ever heard one. How do you really feel?" Dr. Higgins inquired.

"How do I feel? I feel like a Fool! I gave him everything and he didn't respect or deserve it. I was the best thing that ever happened to him and he just walked away like it was nothing to him. Does he realize all that I gave up to be with him? You know he will never find another woman like me as long as he lives. He needs to be careful because you reap what you sow. I pray he never knows the pain that I know, but that one day he experiences the love that I had for him. I loved him enough to let him go and I'm not looking back. I helped him pack and walked him to the door, gave him a hug and shut the door. I made sure that I didn't shed one tear. I wanted him to know that I was going to be alright with or without him."

I was shaking uncontrollably and tears were streaming down my face. But I was finally releasing all the "strength" that was masking my pain. I collapsed on the couch and cried like a baby.

"Why did he do this to me? I would never hurt him like this. Why God, why?" I asked as I sobbed all my pain away.

"That's it. Just let it out. You don't have to be strong here. It's okay for you to be hurt, angry and whatever else you're feeling. Have you had any more panic attacks?" Dr. Higgins paused as he waited for me to gather myself. I blew my nose, wiped my face and tried to steady my breathing as I got myself together.

"WOW! I feel so much better. I needed that. No, I haven't had any recently. I've been praying more and I really believe that helps." I answered him with a partial smile on my face.

"Well of course it does, because you are admitting that you can't do it on your own and you need God to handle it. That's all He ever wanted in the first place." Dr. Higgins smiled as he spoke to me. I was happy that I was feeling better about the situation, but I had another question for my therapist.

"Doc, how do you get to the point where you love that person more than you love yourself? Where you make your decisions based upon how the outcome will affect them? How did I go from pleasing God to satisfying him?"

"That's something you need to think about for yourself. Be brutally honest with yourself. You know the answers. You just have to figure out how the answers will impact the rest of your life. You've learned what to do and what not do and you know how you feel now and how you want to feel. So express those emotions and you'll have your answer."

"And don't just give something short and sweet," he continued. "When you're doing an emotional spring-cleaning you have to acknowledge all the areas. Don't convince yourself that you were perfect in the relationship. You did some wrong too and although yours wasn't as serious as his, they were still mistakes. You just didn't handle yours in the same way that he handled his. People make mistakes all the time and just like God forgives us, we have to learn to forgive others. I'm sure there are a lot of things that he wishes he could do over, and, if he never tells you know that in your heart. Sometimes "I'm sorry" is the hardest thing for a person to say, especially to a loved one that they've hurt. And, although it doesn't make much sense now, in time, God's time, it will. All I ask is that you don't turn away from God. That's a very dangerous move." He smiled and rubbed my hand.

I processed all the information and advice that doc had given me and he was right. He should be. That's what he gets paid to do. But I hadn't taken into consideration all that I had done. Okay. I could be a little demanding. Who am I fooling? I can be a straight up pain at times. But he had a mouth. He should have said something. Being impatient was another weak point, but I was better at that. Yeah. I see I have a lot of work to do. I grabbed my belongings and jotted down a few notes in my journal. I had some serious homework to do over the next few days.

"Thanks for listening, Doc." I smiled for the first time as I was headed for the door.

Dr. Higgins called out "Thank you".

A little confused, I asked him for what, and he said, "For finally giving up and letting God be God."

I snickered. "You are the first person to meet the new me. Thank you for showing me that it's okay to not have all the answers or have everything under control."

While making my next appointment a comforting peace came over me. I knew this feeling. I hadn't felt it in a long time. I couldn't believe how my feelings had switched from melancholy to serenity. My emotions had control of me and I needed to regain my reign. I had mapped out my game plan and it was going to require a lot of me time. I figured that a weekend road trip was exactly what the doctor ordered.

Just what the doctor ordered...

I packed a bag and put it in my car. I would take off as soon as I left work this afternoon. I worked diligently so I could get off early. I wanted to get a head start on traffic. I decided to go to cousin's house in Hampton, VA. I had the keys so I would just let myself in. I could just lock myself in the guestroom. I had my snacks and CDs and my trusty cell was attached to my hip. I was looking forward to this weekend. I would go to the beach and just listen to God make music with the waves while I enjoyed His beautiful paintings of the sunset across the sky.

I had finally realized God's awesomeness one day while driving to work. Now I was so appreciative of all the natural beauties that God has blessed us with. There is no better scenery than the workings of God with all the colors, shapes and sizes.

My Rachelle Farrell CD was on and I had a long way to go. My phone was ringing out of control and I was tempted to cut it off, but I didn't want to alarm anyone. I would give a quick answer and let them know that I'd call them when I get to Hampton. I'm thankful for this highway time because I can allow my mind to wander and really reflect on both the positives and negatives. "Be brutally honest" kept running through my mind as different memories played out the story of my life. I can laugh about some of this mess now, but back then it wasn't so funny. What happened to my jovial sense of humor that helped define who I was? When did I develop such a temper? How did I become so controlling? I really had a lot of work to do. How could I expect to have a healthy relationship without working on me in the process?

I switched on the radio and the Mariah Carey and Boys to Men song "One Sweet Day" was playing. The tears began to flow. Lamont and I used to sing that song all the time and, although I knew every word, I didn't really listen to them until after... No I have to snap out of it. I have entirely too much driving time left and I can't allow myself to have one of those moments right now. A panic attack would really be dangerous out here driving alone. I instantly stopped the car on the side of the road and started praying. It wasn't just one of those prayers where you say 'Lord I need you now.' No. Those weren't going to work tonight. I needed one of those 'you said in your word' prayers to go before Him tonight because only He can help me now. I prayed without ceasing. I had to get that spirit out of that car right now. As soon as I said Amen the phone rang.

"Hello," I said, still a little shaken but thankful for the company, even if it were only for a little while.

"Hey, sis what are you up to?" My boy Mike was on the other end of the call.

"Funny you should ask. I'm on my way up there. I should be there by 10pm." I was cheerful. Mike had been such a great supporter through this whole ordeal. You can never measure true friendship on time.

"Is it Belvy time?" he said, as we both broke out in laughter. "I could always use some Belvedere, Lime juice and tonic water. It does a body good."

"I bet you can." I replied.

"Is your cousin hanging this weekend?" he asked, poking for answers.

"I don't know. She doesn't even know that I'm coming. I couldn't reach her. But I'm sure she'll be home when I get there." I answered honestly. "Are you cooking?" I had to throw that in. Mike was a good cook and I needed a good home cooked meal right now.

"Of course, what do you want?"

"Surprise me," I replied. I love food so there was no wrong choice.

"Not a problem. Call me when you get here and be careful out there. No speeding either. I know how you do!" He laughed, knowing that he drove just as fast as I did.

"No doubt. I'll call you later. Bye" We both knew I was going to speed at least a little bit anyway.

"Bye," Mike said as he hung up the phone.

Thank you, God. You are so good! I had completely forgotten about the song and the on-setting anxiety attack just that quick. I sang, if you can call it that, the rest of the way to my cousin's house. I got there before she did, unloaded my car and let myself in. I took my bags in the room and sat my journal on the sofa. I was slipping. I forgot to get my Slurpee and sunflower seeds. That's usually the first thing I do when I hit the Virginia lines. But I didn't want to stop late at night with luggage in my car. That's a disaster waiting to happen. I headed to the store and passed my cousin pulling in. I called her to see if she needed anything from the store and told her that I would be right back. I was back in no time, but Janae didn't even hear me come in. She was so into my journal that I caught her off guard.

"Oh, I'm sorry, cuz. I thought this was your poetry journal. It wasn't until I had read a page or two that I realized what it was. I'm so sorry for reading this."

"It's no problem. It's not much in there that I haven't told you before any way." I settled on the loveseat.

"Yeah, but reading it is something else, because I can feel the pain that you experienced and I can really relate to it. I knew you were hurting, but I never could have imagined it was like that." She had that sincere look of empathy in her eyes.

A little embarrassed, I just changed subjects. "Mike is cooking for me. Are you going?"

"Nope" she replied dryly.

"Why?" My curiosity was getting the best of me.

"He didn't invite me. You two go ahead and have fun." She spoke without making eye contact.

"He did ask if you were coming. Well, if you aren't going, then I'm not going," I protested.

"No. It is okay. I'm sleepy anyway," she said, making a sorry attempt at a yawn.

"You're always sleepy. We don't have to stay long," I retorted.

"No, Really. I'm good. I'm sure you two will be together tomorrow, too. I'll hangout then." she said.

"I'm going to call him and see if he's started cooking yet and if he hasn't then I'll ask him to wait until tomorrow." I shrugged my shoulders as I reached for my phone.

"You don't have to do that for me." She shifted her pillow trying to get comfortable on the sofa.

"I'm not. I'm a little tired anyway. I can call it a night and start fresh in the morning."

"Start what?" she asked with an eyebrow raised.

"Oh. I have an assignment to do. It is a self-analysis to really learn who I am. It's supposed to help me understand the new me and get me where I need to be," I said nonchalantly.

We were interrupted by the doorbell. "Who could this be at this time of night?" I asked, as I ran down the stairs. Mike walked in and gave me a hug and then pushed me playfully on the side my head.

"I got worried Bighead. You didn't call and it's almost 11pm, so I figured I would come over here and see if your cousin had talked to you." I ran back upstairs and Mike followed. Janae was wrapped up on the sofa which was bizarre, since she wasn't like that when I went downstairs, but I didn't think anything else about it. The three of us sat around and cut up for a little while and then played a couple of games of Phase 10 before calling it a night. I slept like I hadn't slept in weeks. I actually woke up bright-eyed, bushy-tailed and raring to go. I took a shower and with journal, pen and blanket in hand headed for the beach.

The sun was making its grand entrance, it was barely 7am. It was high tide so I was a good distance back from the water. The beach was almost secluded. It was easy for me to find a spot to spread my blanket and get comfortable. There were a couple of joggers running back and forth and one or two children running around, but for the most part it was just the ocean and me. I instantly felt relaxed and refreshed. It was magical the affect that the ocean has on a person if they take time and enjoy it. I grabbed my pen because words, thoughts and emotions were rushing through my head and I wanted to get them all down. I was writing so fast that my hand could barely keep up. I gave up trying to comprehend what I was writing and just let my pen flow. I lost track of time as well. Before I knew it the beach was overrun by hyper children running around, young lovers wrestling with one another and retirees enjoying their golden years.

I smiled as I prayed that I could make it to that stage of life and be blessed to have someone to share it with. "I pray that I understand what 'true love' is and how to appreciate it when it's given without expectations. I know that your love is like the waves that go in and out. You rush in and give us all we need and You take back all the hurt, disappointments and pain that we've experienced and deposit them into the never ending sea of forgiveness. I give me to you God because only you know what my purpose is for being here. Please forgive me for all my sins that I've committed, both knowingly and unknowingly. These and all things I ask in your Son Jesus' name. Amen."

Since I've never been alone, this is an interesting and sometimes uncomfortable state of being for me. I'm so used to having someone that I don't know what makes me happy. I really need to get to know who I am and what I like and don't like. I know what I desire from a mate, but what am I expecting out of myself? What kind of personal goals have I set to attain? I've wanted to be wife and mother for so long that I lost sight of me as an individual. I do know that I want to go back and finish college and I want to have a thriving career, but I don't know in what. I have a gift for writing poetry and I know that my family, friends and church family love my work but is my gift good enough to take me to the next level? I've always wanted to be in a position that I could take care of my family. How am I going to reach that financial goal? I have a lot to work on. Evidently more than I ever imagined.

I thought that I was alright since I got up and went to work every day. But that's no more than a glorified robot. I need more. I sat there for a minute and then glanced down at my journal. I was finally reading what I had jotted down. I read over it once and then just thought about all that I had written. There was some real substance in there. I hadn't really thought about it like that. God is so amazing. I always think that I'm writing for others. But more times than not, when I go back and read my poems, I'm writing for me. That's how God answers a lot of my questions and prayers. I nodded as if God was verbally answering me and then read it one more time. I really meditated over the words.

Be brutally honest...
What happened? How did I get here broken, lonesome and disgusted?
This isn't what I signed up for when God is whom I put my trust in.
I pay my tithes I give my time I do what I'm supposed to do.
But evidently God doesn't view it this way because I've lost my peace, hope
and favor too!
God, I don't get this. What is it? What else do you want from me?
I'm glad you finally asked my child a small voice said to me.
Yes it's true you do all those things but honestly could it be
That you do all those things for you and really not for me!
True you speak of me daily but to me sometime, maybe
And your giving and willingness are attractive
But your heart my dear is inactive
That's what I need for you to be all that you should be
Completely give your heart to me and you will truly see
Because then you will become that living vessel that I desire you to be!
Amen

A comforting feeling came over me as I gathered my things and headed for the house. I'd been out here at the beach all morning. The house was empty when I got back. I wondered where Janae was. I called her cell phone and I didn't get an answer. Honestly, I was a little relieved because I could use a nap. I dropped my bag by the sofa, stretched out and closed my eyes. I didn't even get to slip my shoes off before the door opened. Well, so much for a nap. Janae had been shopping. I hate I missed that trip but that was for the best. I needed to use all my money to pay my bills any way. Since my separation, that had been the story of my life. If it hadn't been for my faith in God and my family and friends, I don't know how I would have made it. If you would add it up on paper, I wasn't making enough to cover my bills but I never went lacking on anything. I truly am a blessed child. Janae laid a bag in front of me and asked if I liked the contents. I pulled out a couple of nice shirts and some pants.

"Yeah, those are nice, but who can wear a size 6?" I asked, a little puzzled because, with the exception of my stress-related weight loss, we hadn't seen a 6 in a minute now.

"It looks like you can. Have you been eating lately?" Janae retorted.

"Yes. I eat every day. I haven't missed a meal in a while." I looked down at myself and thought I was looking better. I'd seen pictures of me after the weight loss and let's just say it wasn't pretty.

"Oh so you're trying to say that I don't look any better?" I asked.

"No. I'm not saying that. But your clothes still don't fit like they used to. Besides, I didn't get you anything for your birthday. So would you please just take them for me?" She smiled as she handed me the clothes.

I got up and went to try them on. They fit perfectly. That's something that I haven't said in a while. I refused to buy those little clothes because I knew I wasn't going to stay a 4 forever. I'm one of those that when I stress I lose things. My weight and hair are the first to go. I have enough hair that I can hide hair loss but I couldn't hide the missing 40 plus pounds. They do look nice on me I thought as I walked up the hall to show off my new threads. I felt like a little child modeling their new school clothes, so proud and happy.

My weekend retreat ended up being just what the doctor ordered. I was able to get a lot of my emotions out and down on paper and I could really feel a difference. That was the outlet that I needed to freely express myself. I could be transparent and open and not fear what people may think. I realized a lot of my faults and I can't believe that I was so controlling. I found myself laughing at how quickly I could flip out when things didn't go how I felt they should. I demanded a lot and I lived by certain rules to ensure what happened around us. I wasn't going to allow my marriage to be destroyed under any circumstances. Somewhere in the marriage I had become his mother and didn't know how to go back to being his wife. I was happy and I convinced myself that he was too. I was blinded by what I wanted to the point that I didn't see what he needed. How sad is that! I'll never blame myself for his infidelity but I can see my part in his frustration.

Why wasn't he able to speak up? I asked that question, but I wonder if I would have listened if he had tried to voice his opinions and concerns. I could be very stubborn at times. By acknowledging my imperfections, I'm learning parts of me that I need God to touch and make whole. I don't want to be some domineering woman that no one wants to love. My goal has always been to be that virtuous woman of which the Bible speaks. The only way I'm going to achieve that goal is to continuously ask God to fix me. If I wasn't trying to become a better person this exercise could cause a very serious pity party.

I could rattle off the positives with no problem, but it was hard to list my negative characteristics. It wasn't hard to come up with the negatives. It was hard because it caused me to admit that I wasn't perfect. I never wanted to be right about everything; I just wanted my life to be in order. I don't like drama or mess, so I figured I would control what was introduced into my world. Being able to write down everything about me, both good and bad, was a startling reality check. Although the negatives were jolting, they were necessary for me to get a true picture of just who I was. This has really given me a good look at myself. I'd never looked into a spiritual mirror and really focused on my reflection. I grabbed my journal and feverishly began to write:

As I look in the mirror to see what you see
I strive to find that servant that I daily try to be
As I think back over my life it often puzzles me
Because I know that you know all that I used to be.
As I reminisce over my thoughts and some things that have crossed my mind
I question whether you choosing me was just a waste of time
But then I study in your word and there it tells me
Lean not unto my own understanding and if it's Your Will it will be
I felt it when you touched my heart I heard you call my name
Now I must surrender all of me and let your spirit reign
This is how you validate me . This is how it should be
I had to experience some things in life in order for you to use me.
Amen!

When my cousin came in the living room I handed her my journal. I asked her to read it and tell me what she got from my writings. Surprisingly she began to cry. I asked her what was the matter and she said she hated that I had to experience the entire ordeal and that she never really knew all of the madness and misery I went through with the separation. I couldn't understand that, since I had told her everything that happened. She continued with her statement.

"I knew all of the things that happened, but I could never even imagine what you went through emotionally. How did you have all of this inside you and not deal with it for all this time?" She wiped tears from her face.

I explained with a smile on my face. I realized that I had my peace back.

"I guess I was feeding off the pain and anger more than trying to deal with my feelings to discover my weaknesses and work on them. Everyone kept telling me that I would be alright in time and that I was stronger than my storm. Now I see that I'm not stronger, but my faith in God was always stronger and that's how I've made it this far. God is good like that. He will hide your faults from others but allow you to see them when the time is right. I haven't felt this good in a long time and I owe it all to God. I didn't do anything different besides listening for His voice. I'm so glad that I recognized it and did exactly what He said to do."

"I think because we were told for so many years that we were the perfect couple that we got comfortable and stopped working towards our goal. We started believing that we were invincible to divorce and when it was a reality we were in shock and sort of just went through the motions. I actually sent my signed divorce papers off on Thursday and, truth be told, it was one of the hardest things that I have ever had to do. I made a promise to myself that I wasn't going to mope around with my head hung low because I honestly tried my best. I have to look at it as if I have been given another chance to achieve what God has for me to do. My future is waiting for me. I just have to figure out what it is. I know what it's not and that's me hanging out in the streets with the wrong people and doing things that I wouldn't normally do. I tried that and it got me nowhere fast. I know one thing for sure and that is whatever I'm supposed to be doing I'm going to seek God's vision and go with that."

We put the journal away and headed over to Mike's for dinner. I couldn't hold back my curiosity any longer. I had to figure out what was going on with the two of them.

"So is there something that you need to tell me?" I asked, probing with my looks.

"About what?" she said cautiously

"About you and Mike, what was up with the robe and the

avoidance the other night? I really don't understand? I thought you two were on your way to a serious relationship?" I just needed to know what was going on.

"Didn't you just say that sometimes everything is not what it seems? We've figured out that we aren't going to work as a couple and we are just trying to find that comfortable place with one another," Jenae informed me after my interrogation.

Crushed by her answer I wasn't ready to get out of the car when we reached Mike's. I didn't want to deal with another break-up right now. I had to mentally prepare myself for what was going to be a stressful night. The one question running through my mind was how could two people that love each other not be willing to make it work? As I unbuckled my seatbelt my once victorious smile was overcome by my now defeated spirit. I can understand my dilemma but these two I can't figure out. When we talk on a one-on-one basis they each profess love for the other. But if I understand this correctly, they don't know how to express themselves to each other.

What can I do other than pray for them? I can't be with them all the time. They are going to have to learn to communicate with each other. I can definitely testify that communication is important in any relationship and without it, no matter how much you love one another, it's not going to work. I climbed the stairs as if I were being led to the slaughter house. When I walked through the door my feelings must have been written all over my face. Because as soon as Mike and Tony looked at me, they wanted to know what was wrong. I put on my best disguise and tried to enjoy my ribs but my silence let everyone know that something was bothering me. I used my own relationship as a scapegoat because I vowed that I wasn't going to say anything about their relationship. I knew they wouldn't question that. I eventually relaxed and concentrated on the basketball game. We decided that we would play cards instead of going out tonight because I didn't want to drive home exhausted tomorrow. We talked trash as the women beat the men and then it was time to go. I must admit that by the end of the night, I had let their little situation go and was once again enjoying my new emotional freedom.

Morning came fast. I had already packed my bags and loaded them in the car. I figured I would catch a little bit of Janae's softball game before I headed home. As I watched her playing her position in the outfield I noticed how comfortable she looked. I realized that she was really in her element out there. I wished she would open up like that to love, but I understood being hurt by someone that you really cared about does cause you to be a bit more aloof. I pray that she's able to tear down the walls that she's built as protection to completely experience what life and love has to offer. Not saying it has to be Mike, but she'll never know until she tries. The innings were coming and going faster than I expected and I ended up staying until the end of the game. I gave her a big hug, thanked her for everything and whispered

"Learn from me" in her ear before I walked off.

"I love you cuz" was the last thing I said as I pulled out of the parking lot.

I turned my radio on as I crossed the James River Bridge. I glanced at my cell and saw that I had three missed calls and one voicemail. I clicked through the missed calls. Two of the numbers where unknown and the third was from home. I called to let my parents know that I was on my way home and then listened to my message. I was stunned at the voice that I heard on the other end. I cut my radio down to ensure that I heard every word.

"Hey, babe. I was just thinking about you. Give me a call when you get this message. Oh, it's me, Joseph."

How wouldn't I know it was him? I've heard that voice for how many years. Of course I knew who he was? I wasn't going to waste my minutes on his antics. I was in this for purging and growing, not playing around.

I deleted the message and turned my music on blast. The weekend replayed in my head until I reached Highway 58. Instantly, I started thanking God for His forgiveness of all my wrong doings and then I asked Him for guidance and understanding of His word. I hummed a couple of songs and then let my mind roam free. I thought about Lamont, something that I often tried to limit. I talked to him a lot in my mind and I've questioned my decision more than a few times. But over all I'm thankful that I even had the chance to have him in my life at all. I wonder how long it will take for me to get over him. It's been over five years and it still seems like yesterday. I miss him like crazy but I know I'm going to have to move on. That's a bittersweet subject for me and I don't know if I'm ready to deal with that part of my life just yet. And I don't know how long it will be before I'm ready either.

I could feel the tears wailing up as I decide I'm not going to suppress them this time.

I screamed, "I'm going to stop trying to control everything and just let whatever happens happen from now on." It was if I was arguing with someone, and in a way, I was- myself. And this time I was winning. It was a cleansing yet exhausting feeling. I know I cried for about ten or fifteen miles. By the time I reached the rest stop I was in full-blown hysterics, and the only person there to console me was me. I yelled out all of my disappointments and made a declaration to God that I wasn't going to allow the devil to steal my joy any longer. I thanked God for His grace and mercy as I let it all out while sitting there for almost an hour. I looked at myself in the mirror in an earnest attempt to get to know this new person. I really needed to get familiar with my new self and understand why I think the way I think and do what I do. My tears had now turned to laughter and I was feeling comforted. It could only be by the Holy Spirit because I was the only one in the car. I got out and walked around to stretch my legs before I hit the road again.

I felt championship good as I jumped in my car, cranked up the radio and headed home. I was smiling so hard I knew the other drivers were thinking that they would love to have just an ounce of whatever I was having. If only they knew that I was just happy in the Lord. I had really talked to Him and completely released everything that I had been holding in. I felt like a new person. My phone rang a couple of times but I wasn't ready to deal with people. I was just happy with it being Jesus and me. I coasted down the highway singing and laughing and before I knew it I was pulling into my driveway.

I grabbed my bags and walked towards the house. I swear there's a camera here somewhere because my phone was blowing up.

"Hello... Hello... Hello... How are you?" I just shook my head. I felt pressure with each call, so I just cut my phone off. I was having too much fun for the drama already. I called my cousin to let her know that I had made it home and I took my stuff upstairs. The house was empty. I wasn't surprised. My parents are never home. I called their cell phones to let them know I was back and then jumped in the shower. I really needed a nice steamy shower to loosen up after sitting for all those hours. I was glad to be in ultimate relax mode. I lit a couple of candles and began to lotion myself down. I drifted off to sleep before I got to my other leg.

Life goes on...

No matter what happens in life, don't quit. That's my new motto. God has a purpose for me and it's up to me to make sure that I fulfill it. But what is it? I ask Him for guidance and I still feel like I'm walking in circles. I am getting adjusted to living single. I even shocked myself by how I've adapted to my new mindset. I do a lot of praying, meditating and writing. I have an appointment today and I can't wait to see what Doc thinks of my journal. I took the day off and slept in. On my way to my appointment I stopped by the Waffle House and grabbed some breakfast. I pulled out my journal to add some finishing touches and to read over some of the very personal things I had written inside. The mind is such an amazing thing. I no longer feel that pain that used to drive me. Somehow I had mentally blocked it out. I would have to look away at times because the pain was so raw in my words. This was going to be a good day and I didn't have the time or need for tears.

I paid my bill and walked to my car smiling, amazed at how different my life looked now. I glanced at my planner and realized that I had the missionary institute at church this evening. I have to read one of my poems since the young adult department is facilitating tonight. I think I'll read "How Long is the Night." It's a bit long but the message is still a good one.

I pulled into the doctor's office parking lot and it was packed. I found a spot near the street and pulled in. I headed for the door and felt this strange feeling. I couldn't explain it, but something was different. I was greeted with a smile as I checked in. The secretary and I engaged in a little small talk before I was ushered back to the doc's office. I walked in and sat down while the doctor finished up some paper work. I sat patiently listening to the soft music he had playing in the background. This office is so tranquil and my mind begins to roam.

I could do this. Maybe this is what I'm supposed to be. I could see myself as a therapist. I mean, really, people have told me that before. Whenever my friends or family need someone to talk to and they want to hear the truth, they always come to me. I was fading into the land of "what if" when Doc asked how my weekend was.

"It was eye opening. I really discovered a side of me that I hadn't noticed." I said excitedly. I leaned forward and handed him my journal, then reclined in the plush leather chair. He held it on his lap as I described in detail my enormous epiphany. I was smiling, almost floating, as I went on and on about the goodness of Jesus. I talked about how I found the error of my ways and had convinced myself that I was in such right standing with God, not realizing my faults. I knew it was only fitting that I rededicated my life to Him right then. I wrote it all down in my journal. I didn't hold anything back. I was so open that it brought tears to my cousin's eyes. I tried to be 100% honest, no holds barred. It was the only way that I was going to move forward.

Doc opened my journal and read over a couple of pages before looking up at me. As I rambled on and on, he said, "D, I'm speechless this is magnificent. The way that you explain the different emotions it's like I'm there with you as you are experiencing everything." Stunned yet flattered at his comments, I stop in mid-sentence and lean over the table.

"Really, do you think so?" I asked.

"Yes, really. This is excellent. I mean besides some minor grammatical errors you have a real gift. Maybe you should look into using your writing as a means to make money," he suggested.

"I love writing, but I never thought of it as a moneymaker. I do read my poems at church and at family functions. They tell me that I should get my material published. But they love me, they are supposed to say that."

"Well, maybe you should consider submitting some of your pieces.

I think you will be pleasantly surprised," he said encouragingly.

I shrugged my shoulders. It was worth a try.

"Where would I start?" I asked.

"If you let me hold on to this until next week maybe I can have an answer for you. In the meantime continue to express your feelings just as you did in here," he replied.

"Sounds simple enough; I can handle that," I said.

We spent the rest of the session going over some of the entries in my journal.

"I'm glad to see that my failures are so encouraging." I chuckled as we wrapped it up for the day.

"You would be surprised at how many others are going through the exact same thing and want to give up every day. For them to see that you didn't give up and you persevered could be that glimpse of hope for them. You are a testimony for a lot of people, believe it or not. They look at you and then their problems don't seem so bad. It's the way that you carry yourself. It's like okay devil, you threw your best shot and yes I stumbled but you didn't kill me. You didn't stop me from doing what God has ordained for me to do." He winked at me as he patted my shoulder. I thanked him and walked out the door feeling really proud of myself. But I was humble enough to know that it is only by God's grace that I have that gift.

I figured I'd head home and take a nap before I have to go to church tonight. I could hear the doctor's comments over and over again in my head. As I asked myself if I could really become a published writer for real? I pulled in our driveway and sat for a moment. Why couldn't I become a writer? God gave me a gift and since it's from Him it's destined to be a blessing. I smiled as I walked towards the house. I went in and got straight on the computer. I had to pull up my poem for tonight. I found it in my documents, printed it out, folded it up and placed it in my purse. It had been years since I wrote it, but I could just read over it as a refresher once I got to the church. I laid out the outfit I was going to wear and set the alarm clock just in case my power nap turned into some serious sleeping.

I swear it seemed as if I had just closed my eyes when the alarm clock sounded. I rolled over to hit the snooze button but changed my mind. I got up, took my shower and got dressed. I grabbed my

Bible and my purse and headed for the church. I got there early enough to read over the poem. I remember waking up in the middle of the night to write this one. I was having second thoughts about reading this poem since some of this doesn't apply any more. Maybe I should write another one real quick.

"It will serve its purpose."

Stunned I looked around. I thought I heard someone talking to me but I was the only person on this side. I pulled my ink pen out and started jotting down words but nothing was really flowing for me tonight. I just shook my head as I struggled to find something to say.

"Read it."

I looked up, afraid to look around for fear of people watching me to see if I was alright. I was so caught up in trying to figure out who was talking to me that I lost track of time and they were calling my name to come to the front. I grabbed my poem and slowly proceeded to the podium and adjusted the microphone. I greeted everyone, cleared my throat and began to read my poem.

Psalms 30:5 reads:
For his anger lasts only a moment, but his favor lasts for a lifetime.
Weeping may endure for a night but joy cometh in the morning.
So my question to God was how long is the night?

Have you ever asked yourself how long is the night?
For the longest time I thought from 8:00 p.m. till dawn was suffice,
Until God opened my eyes and showed me that wasn't right.
My night started in Aug of 97, when God called my special friend and uncle to heaven.
And so I questioned God on many a night
Why when the sun rose I was still trapped in the night.
September came and I found a job, I would tell myself this was my new start.
I'm in a new city and new people to meet
But something was still wrong and my night seemed oh so long.
Man did all he could for his wife that was slipping away.
But no matter how hard he tried I still saw no break of day.
In fact when I saw the sun, tears would stream down my face.
If God loves me so much why does he leave me in this place?
November came and went still dark as it could be,
Not knowing just what God had in store for me.
December 31 I finally gave up,
So to God I gave all of me especially my trust.
My heart was broke and empty and I was just there,
If you would look in my eyes you would find only blank stares.
God touched my heart and filled it with love
And opened my eyes to show me His blessings from above.
He gave me a kindred spirit and a giving will.
He filled my life with a new kind of zeal.
Never could I have imagined life like this, and it began first with a spiritual lift.
I fed on His word and shared with others what I had learned.
Not knowing God was changing my clock without saying a word.
Now morning did not come for a good little while,
Of course the devil still had to hold his trial.

He moved through my husband, my health and my finances too,
But the Bible had already warned me on what Satan would try to do.
So continuously I went to God in prayer,
Remembering to leave all of my burdens there.
See there's someone that God wants me to reach,
And the only way to get your attention is for you to hear my speech.
God can only bless you when you let him in.
God filled the space of my uncle and my friend,
He blessed me with a loving husband, who is also my best friend,
A new career and a bunch of Godly friends.
Gave me a beautiful home and a family with lots of love,
But most of all the ability to see dawn coming in spite of.
So the next time you ask the question "How long is the night?"
However long God sees fit, until you can appreciate daylight.
AMEN,

As a tear rolled down my face I looked up to the sound of applause and a standing ovation. I glanced out at the audience and there were women clapping while some were crying and praising God. This was a bit intense. I had never been the cause of a response like this. What made it even more remarkable was that I didn't know the majority of these people.

I folded up my paper and headed for my seat. I was stopped by women hugging me and telling me 'thank you'. Some said they were going through the same thing and were at the verge of giving up until they heard my poem. They said that I was an answer or confirmation from God. And as I hugged each of them it was if I was taking some of the weight off their hearts and God was instantly casting it away.

Once I got to my seat I just looked up and said 'thank you, God' as I nodded my head. I needed to hear it just as much as the rest of the ladies did. It's possible to get so caught up in what we are going through that we forget that it's not our battle to fight. God has it all under control.

As we were dismissed to go into our different sessions two women met me in the aisle and told me things that I had heard before. But one of them was so reassuring that I knew it just had to be my confirmation from God. I thanked them again and then another woman walked up and hugged me and just began to cry. She told me how she was going through a divorce and how it was affecting her. She said my poem had blessed her and she just had to let me know. I smiled and told her that I would keep her in my prayers. I didn't see her any more that night, but I could hear her voice over and over again.

While in class I was still getting wonderful feedback and I just gave all honor to God. I got the gift from Him so I'll give all the praise to Him, too. I left feeling like I was on cloud nine. Nothing could describe what I was feeling at that moment. I couldn't wait to get into the car so I could call my mom. I was still in reverse, backing out of the parking space, when my mom answered the phone. I was talking a mile a minute telling her about what had happened. Of course, she wasn't surprised. She said they are only telling you what we already know. I smiled, knowing my mom would always be my number one cheerleader. I talked all the way to the house. When I got home we continued to talk until we said goodnight. I was exhausted. It felt like I was sleep before the room got dark. The peacefulness that I had been praying for was finally back in my life.

Nowhere to Run...

All of my therapy sessions and flashbacks were beginning to get the best of me. This was the session that I had been avoiding since Day 1. But to move forward I had to deal with it, and soon. I was reminiscing a lot lately. I was telling the doctor how it was when it came to death when you lived overseas. When you are overseas there's one thing that I think everyone prays for and that is that none of your loved ones die while you are away. Well I wasn't so fortunate. I got the phone call that no one wants to receive. My aunt had passed in her sleep the night before. It was sweet in a way because the last thing she did while on this earth was say a prayer with her young grandson before they fell asleep.

When I heard my mom's voice on the other end I knew something was wrong. I had just talked to her over the weekend and we vowed to limit our phone calls to keep our phone bills down. I screamed out for Joseph when she told me the news and in two days I was on my way home. Money was tight, so I had to go alone. My plane arrived the night of her wake. My parents left the wake to come and get me. Although I was anxious to see my family, I was exhausted. They took me home so that I could get some rest. I figured it wouldn't look good falling asleep at the funeral the next day. I took my shower and turned in for the night. I called home to let Joseph know that I arrived safely and that I missed him. I also had to tell him how much our city had changed in just one year. We talked for a while, but due to the different time zones he had to leave for work. We said our "goodbyes" and "I love you" and hung up the phone.

The next morning was a blur. We were up and dressed and out of the house before 11:00 a.m. When we arrived at the church my family was lining up, but they all rushed to me when I got out of the car. My mom hadn't told them that I was going to be able to come home, so it was a pleasant surprise. To feel that love was going to make it hard to go home, but I knew that this trip was only short-term. It was a beautiful service and afterwards we gathered at my aunt's home. It was night before I knew it and we had to get home because we had church the next morning. To be honest, I was a little apprehensive about going back to my church. It had been a year since I'd seen Lamont and I wasn't sure if that was enough time or not. It seemed like my sister and I talked all night long. The bags underneath our eyes confirmed that. My mom had to come in and wake us up like we were little girls again. I had to admit I really missed this. We were ready in less than an hour, which was record time for us.

When we walked in the church there were mixed expressions. Some people greeted me with a smile, while others were looking with their heads tilted trying to figure out where I had been. But the glare that was so piercing came from Lamont. It was if he had seen a ghost or had never expected to see me again. When we made eye contact a big smile covered his face. A partial smile emerged on mine. I was jittery inside. I didn't know what to feel.

All that was going through my mind was getting out of there as soon as church was over and I did just that. Before he could even get to my side of the room, I was gone without a trace. I was probably on North Tryon before he ever made it downstairs. I didn't want to see him and if I had anything to do with it there wasn't going to be an encounter.

I was able to stay another week. That was perfect because I would be home for our reunion and I would get to see my entire family again before I left. But what was I going to do with myself all week long. Of course, I got to catch up with the Foundation and boy did we have a lot to cover. It was way too much for us to fully discuss on our weekly supervised phone calls, and we had long given up writing one another.

I did miss seeing my sister and cousins and spending time together like we use to. But it was like I hadn't missed a beat by the time we finished talking. Then I had to call up my girlfriends but it wasn't the same. Since I was the momma of the group, once I left they had just drifted apart. I had to hang out with each of them individually. So that meant I heard three different versions of the same story which seemed so petty to me. That's when I said the words I thought I would never say, 'I miss Germany and I'm ready to go home.'

I missed Joseph and me getting up early on Saturday mornings and just riding to see something we had never seen before. I missed our weekend getaways to different exotic spots. And our weekly gatherings with all of our friends where we did more laughing, eating, partying and game and card playing than the law should allow. I missed my friends that are such an important part of my life now. But most importantly I missed my husband, my best friend, my love. I missed our late night conversations that wouldn't end until the sun came up and all we could do was just get up and get ready for work. I missed how much we laughed and enjoyed each other's company.

There are plenty of people that have been together forever that could never say that. Everything that I took for granted was now in proper perspective, even the simple beauty of Germany, with its serenity and cleanliness. I had spent my first few weeks there trying to come back home. But now I was completely satisfied with my decision to marry Joseph and I had no regrets or second thoughts.

The family reunion was the highlight of my trip. I laughed, hugged, ate, played and then ate some more until I was miserable. I was leaving in two days and I couldn't wait to get back home. I saw home differently and I finally appreciated what I had; a good husband who loved me and drama free friendships that helped to make me who I am today. I was able to leave without ever meeting up with Lamont, too. I'm not sure if that was right or wrong, but that's what I had to do. Not only did he still love me, he was so happy to see me that I didn't feel anything good could come out of that. I wasn't trying to hurt him again and I definitely wasn't going to jeopardize my marriage. I slipped out of the country almost as silently as I had slipped in. When I got home I was even more in love with my husband.

I returned to the life that I had chosen. The life I had grown to love. We were traveling, meeting new people and broadening our horizons. Then we got the notice that he was going to be deployed to Bosnia for a year. My stomach was in knots. I was too young to be worrying about this. I didn't want to be over here alone. The holidays were coming and everything was so hush-hush. I'm surprised I didn't have a nervous breakdown or something right then. We had to attend meetings where they bombarded us with rules and regulations. Finally I had had enough. I decided to go back to the states. Back home to the world as we called it, to do my time without Joseph, with my family and friends.

I remember capturing our good-bye party on my new camcorder that I got for Christmas. Joseph found a really nice one for me. And although he would never admit it, he was a little upset because I hadn't gotten him anything. In my defense that's what he asked for, but that's beside the point. I ended up spending Christmas back in Charlotte with my family while he was waiting to board his plane for Bosnia. I figured the year would fly by and we would get our next duty station and everything would be fine. Christmas was on a Saturday and my mom's side of the family gathered for our annual Christmas dinner on Christmas Eve. We spent Christmas Day with my daddy's side of the family. I was dreading going to church the next day. I knew that I was going to come face to face with you know who.

Sure enough, who was the first person that I see when I walk in the church? But this time he didn't greet me with a smile. It was the exact opposite. He almost looked through me. After church he beat me to my car. I slowed my pace to try and get my feelings in check, but my face had to be displaying my nervousness.

Lamont's tone of voice expressed his disapproval. "So you weren't going to call and let me know that you were back in town? Or were you just going to sneak out like you did the last time?"

I just smiled and said "Nice to see you, too!"

He reached out and gave me a hug and picked me up off the ground. I remember the last time he did that I was leaving the country.

"So, what's been up?" I asked with genuine concern. I hadn't talked to Lamont since he called to Germany last Halloween and caused all kinds of havoc. I had to tell him that I was doing fine and if he really loved me he would never call again. He promised and he didn't.

We talked for a while, there in the parking lot. In fact there were only about five cars remaining in the lot when I finally said I had to go and that he could call me later. As soon as I shut the car door Taz, who had been waiting in the car all this time, looked at me and shook her head.

"You know you shouldn't have done that don't you? You are only making it harder on yourself when you have to leave. I can't believe he's still so into you after you told him you were married all that time." My silence answered her question

"You didn't tell him did you?" Taz said.

I shrugged my shoulders. "I didn't see the need to since I was gone. I just told him to go on with his life, wasn't that enough?"

Taz looked in dismay as she shook her head. "What is wrong with you, girl?" is all she could get out before I bribed her with dinner. I really didn't feel like this conversation was necessary and, besides, it's not like that anymore.

No sooner had we reached home did the phone ring and Lamont was asking could he come over. I didn't know how my parents were going to react if he would come and hang out, so I said that I was tired and that we could get together another time. We talked for a few minutes and then we got off the phone.

I went downstairs and sat with my family and watched some of the tapes that we had made in Germany. I had to apologize for some of the language that I didn't even realize was being used, but over all they laughed and were able to see that life was good for me. They were able to see our home, put faces with names and view some of the fun times that we shared. They saw Big Boy from Memphis with the pan of meat hot off the grill and understood where his name came from. They also saw Eric and Suave' cutting up while displaying their different 'Mack' techniques, and J-Rock giving dance lessons while bringing us to tears with his crazy antics. We had our North Carolina homeboy, Michael, who was the baby of the group. I pointed out the real 'Mrs. Parker' before the movie Friday ever came out and I can't forget my sister and brother and my two babies from Virginia. We had the Martin family, our little genius, the computer whiz and my personal chef from the Virgin Islands, who lived right across the parking lot. If I had had more time I could have captured a segment on each member of my new family.

We kept each other balanced. We were a tight knit group that was there for each other and I was going to miss that. I was thankful for all the good times and memories but now I was going to be more concerned with each of them returning home safely. I would be in constant prayer until each of them was home. Watching the tapes was bitter sweet for me because I was able to see and hear them, but unable to touch them, and that was hard to accept. I had my thoughts of how things were going to pan out but only time would tell. I couldn't believe they were laughing just as much the second time and I finally fell asleep on the sofa watching the tape again.

The good part about this was that my mom and sister were off for Christmas break; we went to the malls and spent the day out bonding and having fun. I had sent word in advance to my former boss that I wanted to come back to my old job and he said that he wouldn't have it any other way. So I already had my job squared away and my plan was to save money while Joseph was away. We had agreed that when he came home next year we would have the wedding that our families had complained about missing. I must admit it will be nice to walk down the aisle with all of our loved ones there to share in our happiness, even if we had already been married for three years. I could just imagine the party that we were going to have when we all got together? That's going to be one memorable weekend and I can't wait.

When we returned home I had missed a call from Joseph. I was disappointed, but what was I supposed to do? I couldn't become a slave to the house. That would really be depressing. We settled in and ate dinner. This all felt like a dream to me but it was quickly turning into a nightmare. Lamont just popped up and my daddy answered the door. I called it a nightmare because my daddy called me by my first name. No cute little nicknames today. So I knew he wasn't pleased, but I didn't know Lamont was coming. The whole mood was weird; I wasn't used to feeling this way when we were together. It was if I was sneaking or doing something wrong, but it was all so innocent. We sat outside for a while really saying nothing, just passing time.

Then we decided to go in and as soon as I opened the door I heard familiar voices coming from the den. It was my tape from Germany and I couldn't believe that Taz was watching it again. We had just watched it twice yesterday. Lamont was eager to see what had her so entertained, until he realized what it was. Taz tried to turn it but it was too late he had this look of displeasure in his eyes and I felt the guilt that I had attempted to abandon over a year ago.

"We need to talk." Did that come out of my mouth? What in the world was I thinking? He didn't want to though and I wasn't going to force him. Besides I had a year to provide any information he could ever want. He stayed for a little while longer and decided that he should leave. I couldn't tell if he was upset or just tired, but I wasn't going to pry. I had hurt him really bad and I felt like I owed him an explanation, but, more importantly I didn't want to lose my friend. I walked him to the car and before he closed the door I told him "Thank you, for always being exactly what I needed; a good friend." I reached in and kissed him on his cheek and pushed the car door closed. I watched him pull off and I felt relieved. Although I didn't get to tell him that I was married and that I had been for almost two years, it was like he knew and understood.

I walked in with a smile on my face that worried my parents until I explained what happened and said that I was completely in love with my husband and that I didn't believe in adultery. We had vowed that before one of us would cheat on the other we would just end the marriage. My parents nodded in silence as I walked upstairs. I must admit sitting outside with him did bring back some memories and feelings that I had long since blocked out. I had asked God to forgive me for the way that I had handled the situation and promised that, if I ever had the chance, I would make it right. But I guess when I repented God fixed it for me and I was truly forgiven. Just like old times Lamont called to let me know that he had made it home safely and shortly after that I went to bed.

The next morning I was awakened by a phone call from Joseph. My smile was deceiving. It would have convinced you that he was actually in the room. We talked for about 15 minutes and I must have told him that I loved and missed him at least once each minute. It hadn't even been a week, but I had to be strong for the both of us. Joseph hated to hear me cry and I didn't want to make it harder for him than it already was. The unit was leaving in two hours and he just wanted me to know that he loved me.

"Don't say it like that," I pleaded. "You make it seem like I'm never going to see you again. I just can't imagine my life without you so please stop talking like that." I asked him to do me a favor and, of course, he agreed. I asked him to read the 91st Psalm every day until he returned and assured him that I would do the same. We said 'I love you' one last time and hung up the phone. I must have cried myself back to sleep because the next time my eyes opened it was late afternoon. I had slept the entire day away. No matter how I wished I could spend the next twelve months like that I knew it wasn't possible.

Lamont called, but I didn't even feel comfortable talking to him. He wouldn't stop until I told him what was bothering me. Once I told him he said he understood if I wanted to get off the phone. He told me that was fine, but he wanted me to know that he was praying that Joseph made it back safely. That made me smile because I knew that he meant it. He was that kind of man. I was instantly in a better mood, but I still didn't feel like talking. I got off the phone and took a nice hot shower. I went downstairs and fixed a sandwich and some juice. I wasn't much company today so I went back to my room and just lounged around. If I kept this up I would become a hermit and that was so not like me. It was too early to start my countdown for when I would see Joseph again and I couldn't force myself back to sleep so I started reading the Bible. I prayed for peace first and then I started the first day of a year's worth of reading and believing.

The rest of the Christmas break flew by like lightening and I was back at work before I knew it. Once at work my old co-workers greeted me, as well as a few new ones who were really just trying to figure out what all the commotion was about. It was almost as if I hadn't left at all which was a little eerie. Luckily, I had a game plan. I would work and take some classes to take up my days and the year would pass before I knew it. I had my weekends planned too. I would go to Virginia and see my cousin and everything was going to be fine. It just had to be.

My first day flew by. I prayed that everyday would be like that. And time did seem to fly for another day or two, but after that reality hit and the days seemed never ending. I did everything possible to stay busy, even calling back to Germany more than necessary just to keep it fresh in my mind. I would have never guessed that it would be this hard for us to be apart. Amazing to me Lamont hadn't called in a few days. I was beginning to wonder if he would ever call again. I quickly learned the answer to that question. He was giving me time to deal with the war and being separated from Joseph. He called and asked if I was hungry or wanted to go to the movies or anything to keep me busy. I smiled. It would be kind of nice to get away for a minute. "Come on over." We ended up grabbing a bite to eat and just sitting around talking, actually more laughing than talking. I smiled when I told him that this was just what the doctor ordered and he said that's what friends are for.

We were gone for almost three hours. I knew that I had to get up early in the morning so we headed back to the house but the ride back was silent. Then Lamont looked over at me and asked me a question that I wasn't ready for.

"Why did you leave me?"

Oh, Lord. Where is the blame green light? How did we have such a fun carefree night and then end up on a serious note? I looked at him and I guess my eyes told him I wasn't ready for that particular question.

"I'll make it a little easier for you, did you think of me?"

"Of course I did. What kind of question was that?" To be honest I was still trying to respond to the first question but I wasn't doing very well.

"Do you really want to talk about this tonight?" I sputtered.

"Just forget I ever asked" was the response that I was waiting on but didn't get. So I just bit the bullet and went with my gut feeling.

"Yes I thought of you often but I didn't want to hurt you any more than I had so I figured out of sight, out of mind. Does that make sense?" I pled my case.

"I assumed it would get easier as time went on and I prayed that you would move on. You are a handsome, educated, God fearing gentleman and I know there are plenty of women that would really desire to have you as their man."

An uneasy silence smothered the car again and I was counting the seconds until freedom was possible. I entertained the thought of how my life would have been if I had chosen him, but quickly shook it off. This is exactly why we don't need to spend time together like this. How would I explain this to Joseph that I was just hanging out with the man that I have feelings for? Not happening! When we say goodnight I'm going to have to tell Lamont that we can't do this anymore.

"Did you ask God to lead you before you left?" he asked, catching me completely off guard. I almost fell out the car. Did my house move or something? I peered over at the speedometer and we were really moving, but not fast enough for me.

"You know what I did? I followed my heart. I believed that since we had separated and gotten back together that must have been a sign from God. I believed we were really supposed to be together." I guess I told him because when I looked up we were in my driveway, which was good for me. Another question like that one and I would have jumped out of the moving car. Lamont didn't say anything else. He got out of the car. I opened my door before he made it to my side. I wanted him to understand and I didn't want him to be upset or hurt. But he just gave me a hug and walked me to the door and waited for me to go in. I started to speak and he put his finger over my lips and I knew that we had discussed enough for the night. He said that he would call me when he got home. I said okay and for him to be careful as he walked to the car. He got in and pulled off as I closed the door.

My mind was running a mile a minute trying to understand what had just happened? All I could do was shake my head as I walked to my room. There was no one waiting on me with 20 questions, no missed calls, none of that. It was just my conscious, a room of unoccupied quiet space and me. I felt like I was caught in a whirlwind. I needed someone to rescue me from myself. I lay on my back looking at my ceiling fan and talking to God. I wanted more than anything else to be in God's will.

It was ironic that Lamont asked me the same questions that I had asked myself for months. I felt like I was having a panic attack or something. I couldn't catch my breath. But I quickly relaxed and exhaled a big sigh of relief. I felt released from all my burdens. I couldn't explain it. Then I could hear someone talking to me, but I knew that I was in my room alone. I wasn't nervous. Instead it was peaceful. The voice was soothing and clear and I nodded as I listened to God talk to me for what seemed like forever. I drifted off to sleep under this almost hypnotic trance that was broken by the phone ringing. "Hello. I made it home" Lamont said on the other end as I struggled to respond. He wondered how I had fallen asleep so fast. To my amazement it had only been 15 minutes since we had said goodbye. I was suddenly confused. Was it all a dream or did God really talk to me? I remembered every word that was spoken. But I didn't mention any of it to Lamont, or anyone else for that matter. Instead, I thanked him again for taking me out and we got off the phone. I remember that like it was yesterday.

Almost had you...

Consumed by what I had to do today, I looked at the class ring as I twirled it on my finger. I hadn't worn this in a while, but today was different. I picked out something to wear and I laid back and closed my eyes. I had some heavy stuff to do. My mom knocked on my door and peeped in and asked, "Are you alright?"

"Yes, ma'am, I'm good. Just trying to relax. What time do you want to leave?"

"It doesn't matter as long as we are back here by 5:00."

"Okay," I nodded and sat up on the edge of the bed. I got dressed and walked downstairs. I called Joseph to see how he was doing. We hadn't been away from each other this long in a while. He was more concerned about me, which was comforting for me. I assured him that I was fine. There was a lot going through my mind. I was truly impressed at how well Joseph was handling me seeing Lamont. But he realized that it was something that I had to do, with a little help and explanation from my mom, of course. I told him how much I loved him and hung up the phone. I wonder what Joseph was thinking or if I could be as understanding?

Lamont and I hadn't seen each other in over five months and the last time he wasn't so pleased with me. I'm really nervous but I have to pull it together. We got in the car and headed for the shop but I really didn't feel like going. I tried to talk my way of it, but my mom wasn't having it. We have to pick out something nice and I need your input. I looked out the window and hummed 'One Sweet Day' as we drove around Charlotte looking for the perfect one.

It was actually a fluke that we found it. We saw some displays in the window and I ran in to see what other choices they had. We found one and my mom and I agreed that it was exactly what we were looking for. I sat in the corner as my mom and the owner figured out exactly how much it was going to cost. I slipped off to another place. I just needed a moment to escape the madness, but my time was disappearing.

"D, what do you want to say?" my mom called out getting my attention.

"I don't care, Momma. It really doesn't matter," I muttered.

"Don't start. Come over here and tell him what to put on this card," My mom commanded. I halfheartedly walked over to the register and jotted down a few words put the pen down and walked out the store.

My mom came out in a minute or two. She put her arm around me and we walked to the car. My breathing became labored, but I quickly took some deep breaths and cracked the window. My mom pulled the car over, but I motioned that I was fine. She pulled into a fast food restaurant but I definitely didn't have an appetite. She ordered something for herself and I told her that I would drive while she ate her food. I sat behind the wheel and took my frustrations out on the highway. My mom put an end to that instantly. She made me slow down and I smiled as I eased off the accelerator and apologized. When we got home I backed into our driveway and pulled the key out of the ignition. My mom placed her hand on mine and asked me if I wanted to do this.

"I have to I don't really have a choice." I opened the car door.

"Don't forget that you are a married woman people will be watching you." She said as she got out.

"I know, but I could care less about what others think. They are going to talk regardless," I said. I shut the car door and walked into the house. Rochelle was already getting ready.

"Man, you aren't wasting any time are you?" I asked. I was reconsidering even going.

"I'm sure it's going to be crowded, so we really need to get there early," Rochelle said. She continued getting dressed.

"I really don't feel like going, truth be told, but I would never forgive myself if I didn't," I said. I walked in the bathroom and I took my shower then messed in my hair for a few minutes. Rochelle sat and watched but that didn't motivate me to speed up any. My daddy knocked on the door and told us to come on, but I just stood there. Suddenly I couldn't move. I was too terrified to face what I knew I had to do.

I finally moved and when I got in the car I just leaned against the window. I didn't want to do this tonight. When we pulled up there were people everywhere. This wasn't helping at all. People were looking and pointing, but I just blocked it all out. I just wanted to get this over with. I didn't know what to expect since we had ended the way we did. But whatever happened I pretty much deserved after I had led him on for so long. I really did love him but timing was the biggest factor. He had a girlfriend now and I don't even know if she knew who I was. I walked in and was completely overwhelmed by the crowd. I went blank. I don't remember a lot of it. I was in and out in less than ten minutes. I sat outside for the remainder of the time in disbelief. I was ready to leave when I saw Brandon. We hugged and talked for a little while and then Rochelle came and got me and said we were getting ready to go. I waved to Brandon as we walked to the car. I had only seen Lamont for a short time but he looked good though. I didn't get to say much but there's always tomorrow. Rochelle hugged me as we crossed the street.

My parents talked about how nice everything was but I didn't care about all of that. I'm just glad that the first part is over.

"Did you see ours?" my mom asked to break my silence?

"Yes, ma'am. I saw it. It was nice." I responded.

Taz met us at the door. "How was it?"

"It was nice" Rochelle replied. I walked to the kitchen to get some water before I heading upstairs.

"Is D alright?" Taz asked, like I couldn't hear her. I was just in the next room. I walked upstairs and went straight to my bedroom. I took my clothes off and stood in front of the closet trying to calm my nerves. I threw on some shorts and a tank top and went outside. I sat in the back yard and just enjoyed the breeze. Taz and Rochelle came outside to sit with me.

"Did you see his girlfriend?" Taz asked.

"No. I wasn't thinking about her. There were so many people there that I really didn't see anyone. Do you know how many nights we would sit out here and just laugh at nothing? We would have so much fun together. I never thought that when he left that night that it would be the last time we saw each other." Taz and Rochelle looked at each other and then at me.

"So you didn't get to say anything to him?" Taz asked, still curious about how everything went.

"Yes. Daddy made me go in the room with him. I apologized to him for the way that I handled everything. I told him that I loved him and how important our relationship was to me. And that I only wanted the best for him. But then the silence got the best of me. I would start a sentence but couldn't finish it. So I just walked out and we left shortly after that." I continued to stare off into space as I answered Taz's question.

As I was talking Momma came outside to check on us and to tell us that we were going to have to get up early in the morning to go to the mall. Rochelle wanted to get her nails done, momma needed to find something to wear and I wanted some shades.

I was finding it hard to get some rest so I called Joseph. I figured that he could help me fall asleep. I couldn't wait to hear his voice.

"Hello" he said groggily.

"I can't sleep" I complained.

"Are you alright?" he asked. He was still trying to wake up.

"Not really, but I'm going to be fine," I mumbled. "I saw him. I didn't get to see him long but he looked good. I said a few words but I ended up just walking out."

"I'll be home tomorrow night, babe. It will be better tomorrow," he said, attempting to console me via telephone.

"I hope so. Please be careful coming home." I said.

"I will, baby. Goodnight. I love you," he said in the midst of a yawn.

I sighed. Those three words have caused a lot of pain and confusion in my life.

"I love you, too," I said and slipped the phone on the receiver and rolled over. I was hoping to drift off to sleep, but that was just a fantasy. I ended up reminiscing about Lamont all night long.

Momma came in the room bright and early. I got up and took a shower and got ready to go to the mall. I laid my clothes out so that when we got back I could just get dressed. I didn't feel good. I knew it was just my nerves but I couldn't shake the feeling. I walked around the car until everyone else came out. We were some of the first customers in the mall and we parted like the Red Sea as soon as we hit the entrance. I just wanted some nice shades to wear today. I must have tried on 20 pair before I found the perfect ones. "I'll take these," I said, handing them to the cashier. I couldn't shake this sadness that was causing me to tremble. I was finished with my shopping so I went looking for everyone else. I caught up with my mom first and then we found Rochelle and Taz. We quickly headed for the home. The time was getting near.

I zipped my dress and slid on my pumps. I fastened my necklace and earrings and just stared at this old picture of Lamont. I never thought we would end up like this. I almost blamed myself for the way things turned out, but I know that everything happens for a reason. I was waiting in the living room while everyone else got ready. Finally everyone was dressed and heading out the door when I realized that I had left my shades. I ran up the stairs two at a time and I must have startled my family because Rochelle headed up the stairs after me. I was confused to see her on my heels.

"I was just going to get my shades. Trust me I'm OKAY!" I screamed.

"My bad," she said throwing her hands up in surrender. "Hey, I didn't mean anything, I was just checking on you."

"I know. Thanks, cuz," I apologized. I got in the car and leaned my head back and I closed my eyes. I didn't remember having to do anything this hard before. This was worse than leaving home or saying goodbye to Joseph before he went to Bosnia.

We parked the car and walked inside the church. There were beautiful flowers everywhere. I don't think I've seen this many flowers and people in a church in a long time. I was lurking around the door to the sanctuary. My sister and cousin had already walked in, but I couldn't move. I wanted to move my feet, but they had a mind of their own. I waited for my daddy to come in and Kevin came over and gave me a big hug. He asked if I was I alright and for the first time I told the truth, "No!" He hugged me until my daddy walked over and grabbed my hand. "Come on, Stuff," he said and we walked inside.

I could hear my heart beat pounding. He looked good in his suit and although I tried to stay positive I could feel myself caving in. We took our seats and I just slumped over in my cousin's lap and cried. I cried tears that I didn't know I had. Different images flashed in my mind, which only made me cry more. My cries were soon joined as Lamont's family walked in. You could hear the moans and screams from outside the doors. I just kept asking God why did this have to happen to him? I just didn't understand? The outpouring of love and support just proved what an awesome man Lamont was. I felt so blessed to have had a chance to have him in my life.

The choir sang to my soul and it was the only thing that pacified me while we were at the funeral. I believe I cried the entire time that I was in the church. I looked up as they closed the casket so that I could see him one last time. I wanted to pass out. I was ready to accept that he would never speak to me ever again. I even understood that he may be mad at me for the rest of my life. But I was never ready for God to take him. I would rather have him here hating me than for him to be gone. Senseless would describe the act that took him away from us, but unforgivable would describe how I was feeling right now. I remember my sister and cousin sitting me up and helping me to stand, but I felt so weak I didn't think I was going to make it. As I staggered outside, I hugged different family members and made my way to the family limousine. Silently I leaned inside and placed his class ring in his mother's hand. I mustered up the strength to make it to our car where I just shook my head in uncertainty and disbelief. I didn't know what I was going to do now. I sat with my eyes closed. When my daddy got in the car he asked if I wanted to go home.

"No. I want to go to the gravesite. I'll be alright."

He looked at my mom as if he was questioning my decision, but he followed in the procession against his better judgment.

I sat in the car for a minute and then I found the will to open the door. I stepped out and fell into the pack of loved ones that walked to his final resting place. It didn't seem real. He's not supposed to be laying there in a casket at 23. He's supposed to be living life to the fullest enjoying life as an accountant and traveling with his friends. I heard the pastor saying that it's not for us to understand and that God makes no mistakes, but it doesn't make sense and it's not fair. Why him? What good does me questioning God do? It won't bring him back. If I could just have one more day with him, I could tell him my side of the story. But that wasn't meant to be. As they finished with the acknowledgements and the family started to walk back to the cars I rubbed the casket for the last time and I took one of the flowers from his spray. This was going to be the last connection that I would ever have with him and I pulled it up to my lips and then to my heart. I walked off with my head hung low. What else could happen God what else?

***

Angry with myself because I had agreed to talk about Lamont's funeral in our session I lashed out at Dr. Higgins.

"See this is why I don't discuss this," I hissed as I tried to stop the sea of tears. It was as if I were reliving that moment even experiencing the trembling and sobbing. I somehow snapped out of my personal pity party long enough to blame the good doctor for making me feel this sadness all over again.

"I don't see how this is helping" I said, wiping what seemed like streams of tears from my face.

"It's forcing you to deal with and release your past so that you can go on with your future," Dr. Higgins replied calmly. "Have you ever thought that maybe you can't get over it because you won't deal with it?" He did not even acknowledge my dissatisfaction with having to discuss what I had somehow managed to avoid for four years.

For the first time in a long time there was silence in our session. The good doctor continued to write something on his pad. He was probably writing out a prescription for some Prozac or something based on my behavior today. Right now I can't say that I would blame him. He finally stopped writing and looked at me with a puzzled look in his eye. I couldn't tell if it was disappointment or sadness.

"I need for you to do something for me? I need for you to promise that you are going to let this go. Promise that this is going to be the last time that you harbor all of the negatives of his death and treasure all the good that he brought to your life."

He continued. "I don't care what you have to do but I need for you to do it ASAP. It is okay to miss your friend. It's even okay to get a little sad every once and a while but it's not okay to not deal with it and to keep it bottled up inside. This may very well be one of the most emotional days or possibly weeks that you've ever had because you will actually be dealing with all that you have lost and not just going through the motions." Dr. Higgins peered over his glasses to make sure that I was paying attention.

"I can do that," I conceded as I gathered my composure. "I'm ready for the next phase in my life and if I have to let him go to get there then that's what I will do."

"I didn't say let him go, just let the tragedy go. You couldn't have stopped it. Is that what it boils down to? You blame yourself for his death?" Dr. Higgins asked.

"I did for a long time," I said. "I felt that if I would've handled our relationship better then the ending would have been totally different. I had a horrible dream that something bad had happened to him that Thursday before his death and when I called his home I didn't reach him. I said that I would call back when we got to Charlotte, but I didn't. Joseph and I even talked about going out to that same club that night, but we changed our minds and went home early. That was only God's doing because I can't begin to imagine how it would have affected me if I had been there." I tried to calm down.

"You have a lot of work to do and only you can do it. I'm going to write you out of work for the rest of the day and I need for you to promise that you are going to get some rest." Dr. Higgins's last request was in the form of a demand.

"I can handle that," I said.

I needed that more than anything. My mind was running in three or four directions. I had to just sit there for a minute to get a grasp of what was going on. I made my next appointment and headed for the house.

Downtown was busy and I observed how everyone was preoccupied with being busy, truly missing the beauty of life. The flowers were strategically arranged throughout the city and the water fountains located on either side of the square were absolutely gorgeous.

I drifted into autopilot on my drive home. I was consumed by my session's results and what I had achieved. It was as if the weight of the world had been lifted from my shoulders. I finally realized why I was having such a hard time dealing with my divorce. I had never really gone through the grieving process of Lamont's death. I had become emotionally paralyzed and therefore incapable of dealing with any emotional situations that had transpired. Plus my blatant refusal to discuss, let alone deal with, all of my feelings that I had bottled up inside only stifled my mental recovery and stunted any emotional growth these past few years. I never once allowed myself to cry over Lamont's death after we left the gravesite. So everything that had happened to me since was just accumulating in an emotional storage bin that only God could purge. But I wouldn't allow Him to use the key to unlock all of my pain and heartache. I guess I was punishing myself. That's the worst prison there is- the one without walls that you can leave, but you won't allow yourself to do so.

Once I reached the house I cooked dinner and retreated to my room. I just wanted some me time. I had a lot to think about. I doodled for a while as my mind replayed my day's activities. I never realized how much baggage I had. I pulled out my journal and jotted down a couple of verses and then stopped, looked up at the ceiling before beginning to write again.

I sat there in silence

April 10

I miss your strong yet gentle hands and soft delicate touch,
And those arms that used to hold and console me when I'd had enough,
And those phone calls that went on and on until the sun peaked through
I even miss how you could control me as only you could do.
I miss you telling me you love me, and your actions saying the same
I miss the smile that crossed my face every time I said your name.
I miss the chance to see you at my door or hear you on the phone
And hate that I have to let you go just for my life to move on.
To be honest I miss everything about you from beginning to the end.
I miss the love of my life but most of all, my special friend.
Amen.

I glanced at the clock and remembered it was Thursday. I called my cousin Burt to see if he was going to the track and if so what time would he be there? I looked over at the clock once more and told him that I would meet up with him in an hour. So much for resting, I knew how to clear my mind.

The best five dollars
I've ever spent...

The sound of the gravel crunching underneath my tires notified my mind that I was in my stress free zone. I parked over near the trailer and quickly located Burt. I gave him a hug and joined in on the end of the conversation. He informed me that he had found the perfect bike for me and we all just laughed because I had gotten my hopes up for the last time. I've loved speed for as long as I can remember and I've wanted a bike for years. I figured that now was as good a time as any for me to get one and Burt swore that he would help me pick out the "perfect" one, but we hadn't found it yet. I mean I've been literally sitting on a bike before and he'd ask me if I liked it and once I'd say yes he'd turn right around and shoot it down for one reason or another. The most common excuses were something like "they want too much," or "it's too big" or "it's no good." I understood where this was going. It's just like going car shopping with my daddy. I had long given up on him ever saying okay about a bike and knew that I was going to have to find one on my own.

As we began to walk, I observed what was going on without really saying anything and at that moment my silence was golden. I'm in a man's playground. There were plenty of fast cars, bikes and women. I'm truly in the minority here because I'm actually out here for the races. The sounds from the engines give me an adrenaline rush far greater than any drug could and the smell of Nutech gives me a high that helps me escape from all my disappointments and frustrations. My family has a hard time understanding why I like being here. They don't seem to understand that here I'm completely isolated from my world. I'm not consumed with how my marriage failed or how I lost everything or the fact that my boss is driving me crazy at work but I feel like I can't quit. For a few hours every week I get to retreat to a place where none of that matters and I have some peace in my life even if it's only temporary.

My face had become a regular fixture around here, but very few knew my name. I'm either known as Burt's little cousin, Smiley, or funny enough Burt's girl. I could see them thinking I am his sister since we look alike, but his girl? People would rather makeup something that they believe sounds good instead of asking to find out the truth. But I also understood that there's this unwritten rule that prohibits guys from actually talking to a female that's with another guy if they don't know who she is. No one wants to disrespect, so "hello" is all I say to the ones that I don't know. I guess I can appreciate that. Plus I don't need the drama.

From what I've seen I don't like the rules of these games any way. The guys get to do whatever they want and the women just accept it. If I was going to settle for that I could have stayed and tried to work it out with my unfaithful husband. It's funny to me that these self-proclaimed G.A.M.s (Grown A** Men) refer to how men have had multiple women since the Bible days. They would read that scripture and sum it up as the gospel. How predictable that they hadn't made it to the scriptures that tell you to have no other god besides "Me," or not to covet another man's wife or thou shalt not commit adultery. Heaven knows they don't follow that one. But I'm not here to judge. I just want to relax. I'm thankful for the learning experience too. I should at least be able to detect a few red flags before I fall head over heels in love with someone.

After we passed by the different cliques and stop by a few small crowds that were making a lot of noise we settled in the stands while the cars were on the track. I generally sit back and look at the different groups and laugh because if you would take most of them from this setting some of the same people would be considered lames or even invisible. But in the bike world they are revered and adored. So sad, how backwards is that? But I digress.

I'm startled when I hear someone call my name. The baritone voice is a familiar one. It's got to be G. I smiled as I headed over to give my bodyguard a hug. "What's up boss lady?" he said, a large grin beaming on his face.

I smiled back at him. "Nothing just working and church that's all."

"Are you going to Daytona with us?" he asked. He had an enthusiastic look on his face

"Of course, I've already taken my days off," I assured him.

"Is your cousin going?" G asked, with a sly grin on his face. He had asked a question he already knew the answer to.

"I'm not sure. I'll check when she gets here tonight. Have you seen her yet?" I smiled back at him, playing along the clueless game.

"Nope. I just got here not too long ago myself," he replied.

We both laughed as we hugged while walking back to the bleachers to join the crowd. Rochelle and Kira joined us about 30 minutes later and for another two hours I laughed and clapped while being entertained both on and off the track.

For some reason my phone was blowing up tonight. First Eric called, then Taz. Then I looked at it again and I had two missed calls from Allan. I wonder what he wanted? I'll call him on my way home. It's not like I would be able to hear him while I'm at the track anyway. My concentration was broken when Rochelle asked me if I was going to watch the race. I checked my clock like I actually went by that on Thursday and said, "Yes but only for a little while. I have to go to work in the morning." I smiled because I have to go to work every Friday morning, so what was so special about this one. We jumped in our cars and headed for the street race. Now this was the crazy part to me because we would leave a well lit track and find the darkest road we could and then argue for an hour before we possibly saw a race. We spent the entire time looking over our shoulders just in case we had to make a run for it if the police pulled up. I think because this was so unlike me, I was drawn to it. I've only had to run twice and both times we were out of town. But the possibility always loomed over our heads. I was all for it today. I needed to clear my head. But suddenly I'm completely consumed with "what is next?" I mean I had been going through the motions, but really what was I going to do next?

"Oh man, did you see that" interrupted my deep thoughts. I was glad because who wanted to deal with that on a Thursday night?

"D, you missed it. What are you doing over here?" Kira asked, when I tried to get the latest update.

"I'm not really into this tonight. I'm about to leave," I said, disgusted that my brain was working overtime.

"Are you alright, D?" Rochelle asked. She put her arm around my shoulder.

"I'm good I had an appointment today and we finally discussed Lamont."

"Oh, I see. Are you alright? Do you want to talk about it or not really?" Rochelle knew that these were treacherous waters that she really didn't want to cross. She was with me the entire time the first go around and my crying scared her. When it was all over she said she never wanted to see me cry again. I smiled and assured her that I was good.

I quietly slipped into the darkness as I left the secret hideout for this week. My mind was finally slowing down. The streets were dark and somewhat winding so I had to pay close attention to where I was going. Good thing for me because my mind had already managed to disrupt my night. The journey to my new life requires me to travel roads I hadn't ventured onto in decades. I have thought about things that I had mentally blocked out and vowed to never deal with again. I've whispered things to God that I hadn't said out loud in years, if ever. But these are bridges that I have to cross in order to reach my destiny.

It's starting to make sense to me now. I understand why I act the way I act and feel the way I do when it comes to men and life. It is definitely a fact that I have strong women in my family that have been my role models as I grew into womanhood. But love and relationships have been a weakness in all of our lives. I've not only been a witness but a victim of domestic violence and I made a vow to never allow a man to treat me that way again. I convinced myself that I would control the relationship instead of leaving it up to the man to do whatever he pleased while I just sit idly by as a spectator in life. I wanted to know how to do it all and do it well. I now know that train of thought is completely out of order, but it was still what I accepted as normal.

I figured that in order to move on I needed to deal with my divorce too. I didn't feel like calling Joseph, but I had some things that I needed to say in order to end the bitterness. I sat in front of the computer for a minute and decided that emailing him would be the easiest way to express myself.

I wrote:

Hey babe how are you doing today? I'm doing well and just wanted to talk with you for a minute but we know that's not possible unless I call. I digress.

Have I ever told you thank you for what you did in 01? I know that may sound crazy and I know that it's hard for you to understand because it's hard for me to. I thank you because you stepped out on your faith and did what made you happy. You are in school doing something that you wanted to do and you are at a job that you enjoy for the most part. You have a child and I only assume that you are enjoying your new life. I have been introduced to another life. I think that I wanted my parent's life and really didn't know what made me happy. I'm telling you this today because tomorrow isn't promised. I hope that you have forgiven yourself because I've forgiven you.

I still think about what happened to us and I laugh because for me to be so brave I didn't do it first. I guess I was happy with being safe and content and not necessarily satisfied, and that's a dangerous place to be. I'm not the cheating type so I wouldn't have done anything physical but I did mentally and had the option to leave but didn't take that chance. I still don't like being single but it's better than it was five years ago. I guess we never had a chance to grow up and know ourselves before we vowed to be with each other forever. Now I would have been what I thought was a good wife to you but I see now that I wouldn't have been the perfect wife for you. We see things differently and I thought we balanced each other out, but in the end I guess I was just too controlling. I still feel that the way that we were brought up has a lot to do with it and that's beyond our control.

Any way that's not what this was about, it was to tell you that I love you, I'm proud of you for being a good father and for going to school and pursu-

ing your goals and I wish you the best. I'm working on two books and one of them I'm doing a little dedication to you. The name of that one is *Plan B* and I dedicated it to you because I didn't have one when you left or so I thought. I think that I loved you just as much as I love God and that's a big NO. I serve a jealous God and He never wants to be second to anyone not even my husband. When I get my financial blessing you know if you ever need anything it's taken care of.

What I've learned about me is that I'm a strong woman who doesn't need a man but wants one and that's a lesson that a lot of women haven't learned yet. I make me happy, I love hard and I love helping people, and I'm not perfect. And that's fine. I'm adventurous, I love life, my family and loved ones are the most precious things in life to me. I'm intelligent and I love learning. And I'm fine just being D. God took everything from me so that I could see that with Him I have everything that I need!

Well that's enough for now have a wonderful day!

Keep Striving,

Divine

    The remainder of my week seemed effortless. Now I am truly able to appreciate what I had once deemed a consolation prize, "Peace." Peace had become my new found love. I smiled at the simplest things and I planned to enjoy all that life had to offer. Before I never really understood that it's the small things that matter. Now I'm that bottle of sunshine just waiting to brighten someone else's day.

3 strikes... I'm out!!!

Growing up, softball was a favorite pastime for my family. We would play it on Sundays after church in Cornelius over at the center on the same ball field that my mom and her friends used to play on daily, when she was a child. Sometimes we played in the field right beside my grandparent's house in Davidson. That would draw all the neighborhood children as well as a few adults that still had love for the game. I mean we got so good at it that we would play at Revolution Park in Charlotte bringing along grills and plenty of food once we were older. I was never very good at the game. I just loved playing. I was guaranteed to get on base if I made contact with the ball, but making contact was the hard part for me. I had the speed and the endurance for the game. But my hand-eye coordination was a little less than desirable.

I laugh at that because I see I'm still having some hand-eye coordination problems. My eyes are seeing what they want and my hands are making contact, but my heart and my spirit are striking out in the game. I have to shake my head because you can see signs and hear the truth, yet still have to experience the pain to truly understand what is really going on in life.

Strike one was Allan, my pop-up foul. He was tall, dark and handsome, single with no children, a good job and fun to be around. I was a little apprehensive at first. In the past everyone would always complain saying that I was too hard on men so I just went with the flow. It wasn't a hard decision. He was one of those 'here today gone tomorrow' guys, and he told me that from day one. He didn't like someone up under him all the time and I can live with that. I hadn't had someone in my face every day in a long time so I could have my life and he could have his. He would pop up out of the blue either at my job or at my house. It didn't faze me that much because when we were together we had a good time; but there could be weeks or even a month lapse in between time. I did mention it a time or two, whenever it would bother me, and for a little while things would be on a more consistent basis. But then the inevitable would happen. He would be gone again. Now the Foundation was fed up with him by this point, but I really wasn't pressed one way or the other. I just told myself that's how he was and I kept it moving.

One day Shea, one of my best friends, called and told me that she was at lunch with a childhood friend and they were discussing relationships. She found out that her friend and Allan were in a relationship and had been for years. She made me promise not to see him anymore. I assured her that I had already made that promise to myself and I hadn't seen him in about five months. I have you know that he popped up at my job that very day. I swear my office is tapped.

He's cute I was thinking as I started smiling before I could catch myself. I'm really tripping that he just popped up, as he flashes a smile of his own. I promised that I wouldn't say anything, so I'm looking at him and my eyes are saying everything that I vowed my lips would not. I asked a few questions and just smirked as he replied. I couldn't believe that I was so gullible. He was so natural with it that this couldn't have been the first time that he had cheated in his relationship. But I have to be real with myself, what did I think he was doing all that time he wasn't with me? I convinced myself that basketball and the boys filled in the gaps knowing full well that there had to be another woman somewhere. It wasn't like he had ever taken me to his home or I had met his parents or anything like that. We had become each other's secret getaway when we had a little free time. I was nodding as he spoke. I knew how to deal with this one. I just paid him no attention. I guess that's why he liked coming around me; there was no pressure of responsibility, so he was able to roam around as he chose. I didn't put any restraints on him and really didn't expect much from him.

I'm not downplaying the feelings that I had for Allan. In fact, he was what I needed for the moment. Our experience taught me that I was able to care for a man again. It also reassured me that I didn't have to have one to be happy either. We both came to an understanding that our relationship was unable to exist anymore. I questioned why he even started spending time with me when he knew that he was in a committed relationship? The only answer that he could come up with was that he never intended to develop feelings like that for me. It just happened. Oh boy, those words must be the escape clause for men. Joseph had used them to describe his affair with his child's mother, too.

I scribbled a few words in my journal to practice what I was going to put inside the blank Thank You card that I had bought for him.

I didn't tell you thank you, you showed me that I can still care.
I didn't tell you thank you, you proved my heart has feeling there
I didn't tell you thank you for allowing me to care.
I couldn't tell you thank you, because you were no longer there.

That will work.

Strike two was Jason. He was a perfect pitch, a curve ball that I allowed to sneak by me. Jason was beautiful, if you polled my girls. He had perfect skin and a body that was so enticing that you couldn't help but want him. I was so eager to get another chance at bat that I completely ignored all of the signals, i.e. the recent break up from a long term relationship, or the "world tours" he would make around his house whenever he would get a phone call, and how he was closer than my shadow behind closed doors but then his demeanor was completely different when we were out and about. Besides, I broke my own rule. I never deal with anyone that runs in my circle. I just feel that you should keep certain parts of your life separate. But I didn't take heed.

You know how sometimes you're blinded by the sun when you are up at bat. Well your mind can have the same affect. Your emotions can convince your mind that you didn't see what you know you saw. Or instantly inject past "good time" memories right at the point when you've decided that you've had enough. Honestly I don't even remember what my breaking point was but it happened. There wasn't this big blow up, but we did have a couple of those during our short stint. It was more like a "let's be real" moment and you go your way and I'll go mine, "love you from a distance" type resolution. So I had yet another journal entry. I grabbed my pen and pad and rolled over to write out what and how I was feeling

If the shoe were on the other foot then what path would you take?
Only then would you completely understand some of the choices I have to make.
And although it seems so clear to you on doing what you do
Maybe then you would agree with some of my feelings too.
But only if you are willing to switch roles with me
Then you will truly be able to see the same things I see.

Strike three was Darrel, the slider. What else could you call him besides a slider since I wasn't looking for a man at the time we met? It was the Christmas season and we were at my cousin's annual cocktail party. I was enjoying myself, looking pretty good I might add, with a few affirmations from some of the gentlemen at the party. Then BAM!!! Here he comes. We had a nice conversation in the ladies bathroom of all places and then we exchanged numbers and set a date for later in the week. I couldn't believe that I agreed to go to a party with him and I'd only known him for maybe an hour. He seemed harmless though. And his best friend was one of my childhood friends, so I thought I would be alright.

We had a good time. We spent a lot of time together, but we were just friends. I was cool with that title. I might have been a little gun shy but who could blame me? My track record was a little shaky. We went on long walks, shopping trips and out to dinner all the time, but he was beginning to look for more than just a friend. I remember the jewelry store trip. Now that was funny. I almost had a panic attack in the blame store as we looked at engagement rings. He later apologized. He said he didn't know it was going to affect me like that. I laughed as I told him that I didn't either. He always questioned whether I was waiting to get back with my ex or not. I would repeatedly reassure him that wasn't an option. I just didn't want to rush into anything and he said he understood.

I give him points for his persistence. He waited patiently for months while I decided whether or not he was going to be more than a friend. I threw caution to the wind and went for it. But wouldn't you know it we ended up going our separate ways. He was going through some personal trials and I was just along for the ride. I couldn't believe that I stayed as long as I did, but I'm loyal to a fault. Nevertheless, when it was time to exit I was gone! I tried to be that supportive girlfriend that would help out as needed but then I started feeling used and unappreciated and that I couldn't tolerate. Of course, he made his way into my journal as I made my way out of the relationship.

As winter comes to a stormy end
So does my relationship with you!
As I prune my heart of its disappointments
Life seems so brand new
That smile that's been labeled "Sunshine"
Is yet again peeking through
Mr. Relationship has taught me another lesson
As I reflect over my time with you!

So you know what I'm done. I've decided to just focus on me.

Me...

"Time waits for no one." Literally. I looked up and two years had come and gone. I'd been so consumed with work, school and getting my book together that I hadn't realized just how much time had passed. I was feeling pretty good about the new me. I was active in my church. I had ventured out and was doing more traveling. I was doing well in school and still maintaining at my job. I was a stable self sufficient person. Who could ask for more? I could get up and go when I wanted to. I had the flexibility to do what I wanted, but most of time I did it alone. I spent a lot of time with my sister and my girls but as for a social life well uh that was a different matter. I was tired of all the games and the situations. I was just looking for someone to be faithful and honest and love me for me.

As I sit in silence contemplating my next move, I was seduced by the rain's song outside my window. It was peaceful yet commanding and necessary. It kept time like the drummer in a band while I drifted off to my dream world of who, what and where I want to be in life. It was odd how relaxed I was laying in bed with plenty of things to do but not pressed to do any of them. I was recovering from a week of month end closing at work and exams at school. I could really just lay here and rest, but I knew if I missed Rochelle's party I wouldn't hear the end of it. I still had time for a power nap which would do my body some good.

Three hours later, with the phone ringing nonstop, I finally opened my eyes, rolled over and looked at the clock. I had to hit the floor running. That was a power nap alright. Despite all of my good intensions, if I didn't leave right away, I was going to miss the party anyway. Thank goodness I had laid out my clothes and already took my shower or that would have taken another hour. Tripping over my own feet, all I could do was laugh. I was so pitiful in a funny kind of way.

Dressed, I ran downstairs, out the door and to the car. I jumped in, threw it in reverse and then drive and I was out of there. While driving part of my dream popped in my head. The image was so vivid. I was dressed in all white and my hair was curly. I was extremely happy and I was sitting on a clear globe with the caption "Sitting on Top of the World" above my head. This image brought a smile to my face but I was also curious as to what I had done and how I ended up being on a magazine cover?

Checking the speedometer and mirrors as I bolted down Harris Boulevard, the light bulb went off inside my head. This is Rochelle we're talking about. I know she didn't start on time and besides it's just going to be family up here anyway. I have time. I bumped up the volume on the radio as I hit 77 North, heading towards Mooresville. They are really jamming on the radio tonight, a little Tupac, Biggie, Jill Scott and Lauryn Hill. Before I knew it I was pulling into the driveway. To my surprise there were cars everywhere. I walked in to a sea of faces that I didn't recognize, spoke and waded through the crowd until I reached some familiar folks.

"Who are all of these people?" I asked, as I walked in a circle hugging all my family.

"Some of Rochelle's friends," Taz commented. She shrugged her shoulders and walked in the kitchen.

"What did you do, over sleep?" Kira asked as I gave her a hug.

"You know me so well," I giggled. I walked over to the sofa to sit down.

"So what's up? What did I miss?" I inquired. Since they were all gathered in one spot I figured something was up.

"Nothing, just sitting here laughing at the entertainment," Taz said. The look on her face said all that her words didn't.

"I see," I replied and began to scan the room to see who was performing at that moment.

"So how's the book coming along?" asked Kira, who sipped on a daiquiri.

"Girl, I'm tired of reading and writing," I sighed, and we all chuckled. "But it will be worth it in the end." I smiled while trying to visualize my dream again.

"So how much longer do you have?" Taz asked.

"I don't even want to put a date or time on it anymore. I thought I would be finished by now and I'm still working. So I'm just going to say I'll know when it's done." I winked and smiled.

"So who are you seeing now?" Kira asked

I didn't respond because I assumed she wasn't talking to me. I was fixing my plate when Kira called my name.

"D, I'm talking to you." She motioned with her hand for me to spill the beans.

"Don't make jokes while I have food in my mouth." I said starting to laugh. "I can't even remember the last time I was on a date. I never thought I would be saying that. Oh well, it is what it is." I picked up another meatball and shoved it into my mouth.

"She won't meet anyone sitting at my house every weekend" Taz spouted like her social life was all that.

"Whatever, social butterfly." That statement caused the room to erupt in laughter.

"Let's not turn this into a meeting at the round table tonight. Let's save that for another time and another place," I pleaded, as some guy walked through the kitchen.

"Point well made," Rochelle sang as she came in and pulled me into the living room.

"Look who's here," she whispered, pointing towards the door.

I could feel that simple little school girl smirk on my face as Miles walked in. I was so over that little arrangement, but I think the sneakiness of it intrigued me. I stood there in the middle of the living room as he made his way towards me. No butterfly moments or anything like that, but no harbored ill feelings either. We were cool for lack of a better word. Just cool.

"Hey" he whispered in my ear as he gave me a hug.

"Hey, how are you?" I answered, not too excited, but not dry either.

"I'm good, where have you been hiding? I haven't seen you at the track or anywhere?" Was he trying to convince me that he genuinely missed me with his tone?

"Church, work and school. That's it for me," I answered still sniffing his cologne and internally laughing at myself while trying to stay focused.

"You're looking good as always." He smiled, looking me up and down.

"Thank you. I'll see you later," I said, as I walked off not impressed by his latest move.

As I walked away I was quite impressed with the way I handled my little encounter. I really didn't know what to expect. I hadn't seen anyone from my past in a while. I've been too busy trying to move forward. But that's a good thing. If I had continued doing what I was doing I would have only hurt myself.

I positioned myself at the card table and that's where I spent the remainder of the night. It was a typical house party, a lot of laughing, a couple of smoke-filled rooms and some alcohol. That pretty much summed it up. I see I'm not missing anything "in the world." I found myself riding home with my windows cracked and mad because I knew I was going to have to wash my hair to get rid of all the cigarette smoke. I just don't see what people get out of smoking, but hey everyone has their vices. I backed into the driveway and just sat there for a while before I got out of the car. Looking at the stars and listening to some music was so peaceful. The rain had stopped and raindrops glistened on blades of grass in the moonlight.

Before I knew it, the sun was peeping through. I snapped out of my trance and grabbed my things and ran in the house. I was determined to be in my bed asleep before the sun came up. I pulled the comforter over my head too late. I was caught. The sun was beaming and no matter where I placed my head, I couldn't hide from it. I figured if I laid there long enough that I would drift off to sleep. I could hear my parents stirring around in the hallway. I tossed and turned until the next thing I knew it was 2 o'clock in the afternoon. I sat up in the bed still not ready to commit to starting my day and just looked at myself in the mirror. I knew what I had to do, I had to get back out there and start dating again. I can only find so much busy work before I run out of things to do. I took a deep breath and slid back underneath the covers and was out like a light.

Tick Toc...

The next few months happened so fast. It was like I checked my calendar and the year was almost over. My job, which had begun to burn me out, had been taken over by another company that promised to be as different as night and day. I had to leave school for financial reasons, with a personal promise to complete my degree by the time I'm 40. And I'm still single. So I must say that my life has been challenging lately, but doable. I had to put a few things in perspective so that I didn't end up back at Square One. But, hey, I'm a trooper.

I love my new job, all of the promises that had been given beforehand were actually valid and I enjoyed going to work again. I could breathe now that the pressures of bad management and favoritism were a thing of the past. I just needed to get my schedule situated so that I could return to school and I would be back on target. I was even still able to meet with Dr. Higgins once a month, which I enjoyed. My sessions were more of a mental maintenance than anything else. I continued to share my journals and work on my book. Dr. Higgins made subtle suggestions in certain areas that I mentioned in my writing but for the most part he was pleased with what I had produced. Not only for its book value but also for what it helped me to accomplish by letting things go and allowing the past to be the past.

I had a big bomb to drop on him today; I want to have a baby. I know it's going against everything that I stand for as far as family structure, but I'm not getting any younger and I don't see suitors climbing over top of each other to marry me either. I even mapped it out and have mentioned it to a few, well, three to be exact, guys that I know very well. Although they looked at me like I had three heads, I'm sure I can persuade one of them to go along with my plan in time. I strutted into the office "Ms. Happy-Go-Lucky" ready for today's session. I spoke, signed in and waited patiently for my name to be called. While waiting, I silently practiced my announcement until I heard my name. I smiled as I looked up and saw the familiar face and grabbed my things.

"Hello, D. How are you doing today?" Dr. Higgins greeted me as we walked to his office. "I'm doing great and I have some good news," I answered, so proud of what I was about to say.

"Is that so? Well, that's wonderful. And to what do we owe this great day?" he said, smiling from ear to ear anticipating what he thinks I'm going to say.

"I'm ready to have a baby!" I was ecstatic about my statement, but based on the grim look on Dr. Higgins' face, I was the only one.

"Come again. You're ready to have a baby? But you don't even have a boyfriend, let alone a husband. Unless there's something you forgot to tell me?" His facial expressions showed that he was confused by my announcement.

"Well, yeah, I know that, but that's the one thing that I really want and I'm not getting any younger. You do understand where I'm coming from?" I asked, almost begging for his approval.

"I understand how you are feeling, but I don't think you're separating your emotions from a life changing decision that once you've made it there's no turning back," Dr. Higgins said very politely.

I sat silently in my seat waiting for Round 2, because that was too easy. I knew he wasn't going to just let me leave with that tidbit.

"So what did the potential fathers say?" he inquired.

"Well, not what I expected. I told them, them being the three men that I mentioned it to, that I just felt like it was time for me to be a mom. I assured them that I wouldn't need them for anything besides the obvious. All they had to do was make the donation at the clinic and walk away. I would even draw up a contract to relieve them of any financial responsibilities and all paternal rights." Hearing myself as I'm telling him how it played out I realized that it does sound a little crazy.

"Uh huh, well let's see. I'm guessing based off what you are telling me, that you feel as if your biological clock is winding down?" he questioned, trying to see what position I was taking before he made any comments.

"Yes. No. What I'm saying is that I always said I wanted to have a baby by the time I was…" and I stopped in mid-sentence and realized that I was doing it again, trying to plan out my life the way I felt that it should go. Dr. Higgins just sat there with a partial smile on his face. It was the type of sympathetic and understanding grin that didn't make you feel foolish, but let you know that you just stopped yourself from making a huge mistake. He had caught me before my world went spiraling out of control and there would be nothing anyone could do to fix it. We spent the remainder of the session just talking about life and how what God has in store for us is far greater than what we can imagine. He reached over and squeezed my hand and told me to relax and enjoy life for what it is day by day and things will happen when they are supposed to happen. He skimmed over a few of my journal entries and we discussed the book some and it was time to go.

Stunned by how easy it was to slide back into "control my own destiny auto pilot" I just shook my head with disappointment as I drove home. I was too embarrassed to tell anyone what I was planning. And now that I had heard how ignorant it sounded as I said it aloud, all I could do was talk to God. But I wasn't in a praying mood. I was too outdone. I keep saying I'm going to let go and let God but I keep trying to handle it or fix it myself. "God what is my problem?" I screamed out in the car as I traveled along North Tryon. I didn't want to hear any music and I left my cell phone on vibrate. The car was silent other than the humming of my engine. Quite enough for me to hear "Am I your source? If you say I am then let me be!" I quickly look to my left and my right. I didn't want the people in the cars beside me to think I was crazy. I turned the music on and started to sing as loud as I could, while still looking out the corner of my eyes checking as if someone else could hear what I heard.

When I got home I walked in the house, spoke and marched straight upstairs. I dropped my purse on my bed and fell face first into the mattress. I realized that I was my own worst enemy. I just called on God and asked for help. I remained facedown, arms stretched wide until my mom called me downstairs for dinner. I went to the bathroom to check my face. I had been crying and my face would tell on me, so I played like I wasn't hungry. I figured that I would eat something later. But that was just a red flag for my mom. Me turning down some food is not going to happen. That doesn't happen unless I'm stressing out. My mom tapped on the door as she was pushing it open. "Are you alright? You haven't said a word since you came home."

"Yes ma'am" I answered in that' I just woke up' voice trying to throw her off. She wasn't buying it though; she flipped on the light and saw my tear stained eyes. With that motherly concerned look in her eyes she came over and gave me a hug and kissed me on my forehead, turned back around, cut the light off, shut the door and walked back downstairs.

Shocked and mildly impressed that she didn't ask any questions, I just sat in the center of my bed in the dark. I could hear my parents muffled conversations, but I couldn't make out all of the words clearly. I could hear my daddy saying something like, I would be alright, but other than that I couldn't really hear them. I tried to wait them out, but it seemed like forever and I was getting hungry. So I just bit the bullet, got up, went to the bathroom washed my face and hands and headed downstairs. My parents didn't move an inch when I walked into the kitchen. Some television show had their undivided attention and I was able to get my food and eat without the inquisition. After dinner I sat at the computer playing games online to mentally relax. Then I typed a couple of pages for my book. Before long I was sitting in the living room watching television with my parents and everything was fine.

I remembered that I hadn't washed clothes this week and I was going over to Taz's house for the weekend so I decided to get started. I was just starting my first load when Burt called. They were racing and he wanted to know if I wanted to come. No need to say anymore, I was on the way. I finished separating my piles, grabbed one, tossed it in the washing machine, hit the start button, kissed my parents and I was out the door.

Once I was out in the fresh air I instantly felt better, not a care in the world. I pulled into the parking lot where everyone was meeting and got out to do my parade of hugs. It had been a while since I had been out and I was actually a little excited to see everyone. The first person I hugged asked me if I were married yet or had any kids, since they hadn't seen me in a while and to my surprise that made me laugh. That was one of the best nights that I've had in a while, just having fun, nothing intense. Just plain old fun. I believe I got home around 2:30 in the morning. Sadly confirming that I'm getting too old for these late night excursions as I opted to sleep downstairs too tired to go up to my room.

Mister

December 17, 2005 didn't seem out of the ordinary for the president of the "sit at home and wait until God sends him" club. But little did I know God was really going to do it. I was going to open the door and my Mr. Right was going to be standing on the other side. I wasn't the only one surprised. He thought he was being dragged over to meet the meanest woman in Charlotte. But he was pleasantly surprised to meet a beautiful, intelligent, misunderstood woman who just wanted to be loved and adored by a faithful man.

That seemed like yesterday to me, but it has been a couple of years now. As I lay beside him in the dark being serenaded by the sweet sound of his breathing, as he slept peacefully, I smiled. Not because of anything that we had done, but from the things that we had discussed. He was so different from my perception of him. His calloused hands were from years of honest hard work, not from wasting time hanging out in the streets. His wisdom didn't come from years of higher education but from this institution called life. He taught me something new all the time. Things that really mattered in life, like kindness and genuine gratefulness for the things that God had blessed us with, just because. I took every lesson to heart because I wanted to be that good woman that he thought I was and that I knew I could be. He made me better.

The funny thing was that I was the one that spent countless hours in church and doing "God's work" while he was just living. I looked at him in amazement because somewhere I had missed the mark. The pure accomplishment of being a good person was my ultimate goal, but I got in the way by getting caught up in the formalities of it all. What I should do, where I should be and who should I be with. God looks at our hearts and he figured that out long before I truly accepted this principle. It's not about the good that I've done or about whom I've helped. It's about my heart and my obedience to God.

My life had changed since I met him. I no longer worried over the small things; I just lived day by day and enjoyed life. I was back in school and I had finally finished writing my book. He was one of my biggest cheerleaders and I love that. I pecked him on his lips and I rolled over to go to sleep. The morning crept up on us in a flash. I rolled out of bed and got ready for work. I kissed him good-bye as I headed out the door. As I was pulling out of the driveway my cell phone rang. I grabbed it and noticed that it was Dr Higgins on the other end. I answered a little confused because I didn't have an appointment today but he answered all my questions with two sentences.

"Hello, Dr. Higgins."

"Good morning D, I have some good news for you. I would like to meet with you today so we can discuss getting your book published. How does that sound?" he said.

"Don't play with me. Are you serious?" I could barely contain myself.

"Very, do you think you can come by today?" he continued.

"What? Do I think? I'm getting ready to call my job as we speak" I said.

"Slow down. There's no need to fly over here. I have a couple of appointments this morning and I have to contact Tom to see what time is good for him".

"Okay, I guess I can go in for half a day." I said, laughing at myself as I drove down the street.

"That's better" Dr. Higgins said chuckling at my response.

"I'll call you in an hour." I said, as we got off the phone.

I couldn't believe it. It was really coming into fruition. I was going to be a published author. I needed to call my parents, but of course they are at work and so is Taz. I looked up and gave a quick 'Thank you God' praise and called Will to share the good news.

"Babe," I was screaming by this time.

"What's wrong, babe?" he asked apprehensively.

"No, there's nothing wrong. It's what's right. Dr. Higgins just called me about my book." I was too excited to calm down.

"Really, babe. That's wonderful. I'm so proud of you." I could hear him smiling.

"I know, right. But now I'm nervous." a little embarrassed to say it aloud.

"Nervous about what?" he questioned.

"Failing" I mumbled.

"Are you serious? You fail if you don't try" he quickly replied.

I was silent for a few moments and then I continued.

"I know you're right, but that's still what I'm feeling" I said defending my feelings.

"I don't want you to say that to anyone else, do you understand me?" he said sternly.

"Who are you talking to?" I screamed on the defensive.

"Why are you yelling?" he said calmly.

"Because, I don't know. I guess because you are right and I didn't want to hear it. I don't know." We both started giggling.

"My baby is an author," he said proudly.

"I know, right. Hard to believe isn't it? Growing up I never would have thought of writing as my career." I chuckled, "You know I can't spell"

"I always knew you could do it. You have a real gift." His affirmation made me smile.

"Thank you." I said, grinning from ear to ear.

"But, Ms. Author, you're going to be late, and you aren't getting paid to write yet so you better get to work." he said with a laugh.

"I know that's right. Before I'm holding a, 'Will Write for Food sign." and we both laughed.

"Have a good day, baby, and congratulations on your book" was how he ended our conversation.

"You too, sweetie. I love you" I kept smiling as I hung up the phone.

I whipped my car into the employee parking lot and grabbed my badge. I was mentally running down all that I needed to do before 1:00 and the list kept growing. I ran into Anne's office and told her my good news. Then I asked Rick if I could work a half day and told him why I needed to leave. He had no objections. So I called Dr. Higgins and asked if 2:00 was good for them and he said that would be perfect. I diligently worked until noon and then my mind got the best of me. I was thinking of how my life was about to change and how I would be in a position to help others once I was successful, and what I was going to wear on Oprah. Then I found myself laughing because I hadn't printed the first page yet and I was already answering interview questions on Oprah. There's nothing wrong with dreaming though it keeps my mind active.

I finally got in touch with my family and we were screaming and praising God because it was happening. What a difference time makes. Less than six years ago I didn't want to live another day and now there aren't enough days to accomplish all that I want to do. I headed over to the office to meet up with Tom and the doctor. Tom was a good friend of Dr. Higgins who owned his own publishing company. Dr. Higgins had given him a sample of my writing and he was interested in seeing more. I noticed that he had two proposals lying on the table as I sat down. I reached for one of them as he expressed how willing and eager he was to work with me.

"I've heard nothing but good things about you," he explained as he reared back in the seat.

"The same here and I hope to know firsthand," I said.

"I read some of your work and I'm impressed," Tom said with a smile on his face.

"I brought my manuscript if you would like to read more," I said and handed him the binder. He placed it on the table.

"I've read enough to know that you have a talent and I'm here to help you get it out to the world." He answered.

Speechless and smiling, I just sat in awe. He was saying all the right things, but I had been excited before with other publishing companies and nothing happened.

"So what does that mean? What will I need to do?"

"Be hungry and ready," he said with confidence. "If you can do that, I can handle the rest".

I was hooked. At this point whatever he said was good with me. I jotted down a few notes and placed the proposals in my portfolio and three hours later was out the door.

So elated by the days' events, I'm not really sure how I made it to my driveway but I was home. I jotted a couple of notes on the first few pages and then started editing my book. I want my manuscript to be as close to perfect as possible when I hand it over to Tom. I placed the proposals on the coffee table so that I could go over them later. I needed to find an attorney because those contracts were Greek to me. I called my girl Tia to see if she knew of any entertainment attorneys and told her what had happened to me today.

Two heads are better than one...

"I told you it was going to happen" my writing partner, and one of my closest friends, said as she congratulated me on the meeting. We vowed to encourage each other until we completed our books; that was two years ago but we didn't quit. I would be lying if I said that we didn't get discouraged or even take a writing break or two, but we didn't quit. I was so ecstatic I could barely finish a sentence. I rambled about my book release party and my plans to open a publishing company and we would get excited all over again. We talked well into the night and actually came up with a lot of great ideas and even some new topics for future books.

We discussed God's plan for us and how we were destined to do well because God never fails. He had given us this gift for a reason. But we were stuck on one thing. How do we classify our books? I didn't want to lock it into just one genre because it's not just for one set of people. Plan B's concept could help anyone. The situation could be a relationship, a job, a business, anything that we set out to do. If we don't seek God's vision for us we're doomed from the start. I had no clue how to tackle this decision. I just knew that I was writing a novel and that I needed to get it out for any and everyone to read. It was bigger than color barriers and age restraints and it was easy enough for anyone to understand.

"Write the vision; make it plain," Tia chimed in as I was talking and we both giggled. That was easy for us to say but difficult for some to comprehend. Hindsight is always the greatest guide but I didn't want my book to come across like I was preaching or anything like that. I just want people to know that you don't have to go through all the heartache and pain if you just go to God first. Instead we try doing everything alone, based off what we want and think we need. We make life so much harder than it is but for some reason we continue to do the same thing over and over again.

Switching subject from me to Tia, I wanted to know how her project was going.

"So how's your book coming along?" knowing that we both need that extra push, when it came to setting aside some time for writing.

"Oh it's coming" Tia replied, which was code for I hadn't worked on it in a while.

"Well, send me the latest section," I stated, which meant I was on to her.

"Girl I haven't really done a lot with it, but I did come up with a couple of scenarios," she giggled knowing she was busted. As she laid out her ideas I sat in amazement. She had such a gift and as she explained it to me I could actually see it in my head. I thank God my pastor took us to lunch that afternoon. If he hadn't we'd probably still be saying "hi" and "bye" in passing at church. She was one of my closest friends and I had known her the least amount of time. But ever since that day we've had some sort of bond that I wouldn't trade for the world.

The publishing process was going to take a little while but in the meantime we were going to get the book release party together and come up with some marketing ideas. This proved to be a little harder than anticipated because neither of us had attended a book release party before. The first thing to tackle was a budget and a guest list. That was going to be a nightmare in itself because my family is so large and I know a lot of people. We threw figures back and forth until we came up with a reasonable budget. Selecting a location was going to be another issue. Where can I find a nice place to accommodate my entire guest list and not cost me an arm and a leg? I have to keep in mind that my budget includes catering costs. I want to provide some type of refreshments. Entertainment is another concern; do I have a live band or a DJ or both? Tia reeled me in. She could see my big ideas just demolishing the budget in no time. I told her that I was going to set up a time for all of my girls to get together so that we could get this together. I know when we put something together it will be nice. We talked for a little while longer and then got off the phone.

I am so thankful for my girls, for my support system as a whole. I never would have made it without them. God had put each one of them in my life for a reason well before I understood what it was. I started jotting down things that I would like to express to everyone at my party. I would have all of my loved ones in place at one time celebrating a wonderful milestone in my life, what better way to show my gratitude for all that they have done for me and just how much I truly appreciate them? I wrote a little more and then closed my tablet. I sent out a text to my girls to set up a meeting so that we could get this party together and go shopping to find me that perfect outfit. My cell phone was beeping out of control; before I knew it, I had ten confirmations.

I could feel the tears welling up in my eyes. If you would have told me about this the day, after Joseph's announcement seven years ago, I would have told you to take a hike. But look at God. I was on my way to completing my accounting degree, I was publishing my first novel, I was doing well in my career, I was in a loving relationship and I was happy. Not only am I happy but I have peace, and that's worth more than money can buy. The love and prayers from my support system kept me when I wanted to give up and my relationship with God sustains me daily.

Believe!!!

Smiling, as I look in the mirror, all I can think is God is so good! Seven years ago I wanted to give up on life and today I'm having the time of my life. I was actually fortunate enough to get a second chance to fulfill my life's dreams and aspirations. Who else but God could do that? Who else could create in me a new spirit and zeal for life other than Him? I was jaded and bitter and at my wits end but I had that seed of faith inside me that wouldn't allow me to give up. Now I'm getting dressed for one of the biggest events in my life. All of my loved ones are going to be here to help me celebrate the release of my new book. Who really thought that I was going to achieve that goal? To be honest, I was little leery but life has taught me to live by faith and not by sight.

I still haven't decided which dress I'm going to wear. I can't wait for everyone to see me. They are going to be amazed at how different I look. Finally my mom can be happy, I'm wearing makeup just for her. For me the shock value alone is going to be priceless. Will is going to love this one as I finally decide which dress to wear. You know my boys are going to show out. I can count how many times they've seen me in a dress. I can't wait for Mike to get here. He's the last one. Everyone else is at the hotel getting ready and I can't be late for this one. How many times does a person get to have all of this while they are alive? This is truly a blessing. I exhale in pleasure and excitement. I haven't felt like this in a long time. I slip on my heels and walk into my room. Moni starts to tear up.

"I'm so proud of you, D." and she rushes in to hug me. We squeeze each other and I can feel my emotions getting the best of me but they are tears of joy not sadness. Besides since Moni is the makeup artist who cares if I mess it up. She can fix me.

"I'm blessed," is all I'm able to get out before the Foundation burst into the room.

"Oh, my God, you look great." Rochelle screams as she runs towards me. I'm blushing uncontrollably. I could get use to this.

"So what are you trying to say? I look a mess any other time?" I asked, teasing her.

"No, that's not what," Rochelle tries to clean it up before she's interrupted, Taz jumps in.

"No, not a mess, a hot mess! You know you would throw on some stuff sometimes and we would look at you like, "what in the world," but you were doing you so we just kept it moving."

We break out into laughter because that was true. I have been known to just grab something and go. We looked around the room filled with every kind of flower I could name. Taz complained that it smelled like a funeral home, but I thought it smelled like love!

"Okay, Diva we're going to let you have your night trying to show us up with that beautiful dress and all, but you know you're going to have to keep it up, don't you?" she said cutting her eyes over at me.

"I'm going to think about it!" I said, knowing full well that I couldn't and wouldn't go back to my old ways. I was only moving forward from this point in my life.

"What time is it? We better get out of here. I don't want to be late for my own party." We gathered our things and headed for the door. I told them to wait one minute I had to get my journal.

"Tonight can you just enjoy the moment? If it's that serious, you'll remember it when you get home," Taz said. She looked towards the ceiling to show her annoyance.

"It will only take me a minute. Don't worry. The guys will still be there when we get there."

Moni smiled. "He better be!"

"He! You're still trying after all of these years?" Taz said jokingly.

"I'm going to make it happen this time especially since he's just three hours away now?" Moni answered, still smiling. "I'm not just talking about him. I'm talking about them in general"

"'He' sounds real specific to me," I insisted.

"Whatever, just hurry up!" Moni said.

"How are you going to rush me on my day just for that...," I paused.

"D, come on. You'll be mad if your party starts without you." Taz jumped in to save Moni.

"Oh shut up Taz! You always want to run something. I'm coming." I said, as I marched down the stairs. "I'm ready"

"Finally" Taz said as we walked out the door.

The limo was ready to go and as we were getting inside I had a flashback to the last time we were all climbing into a limo and I just smiled.

"What are you thinking about that has you smiling like that?"

"God's grace and mercy" I replied.

"I know that's right," Rochelle hollers out as we ride down Harris Boulevard.

Three different conversations erupted as we were chauffeured to the party and when we pulled up the view was better than I could have ever imagined. There were cars everywhere and people were even outside waiting to get in. We all started screaming and nearly caused the driver to wreck. After we begged him for forgiveness, we invited him inside. I wanted everyone to be a part of my big night. He was ours for the next six hours anyway he might as well have fun instead of sitting in the car waiting for us to come out.

They rushed me in and quieted the crowd so that I could make my entrance. I was waving like I was in the Carousel Parade or I had just won the Ms. America Pageant or something. I was amazed how they had decorated the place. There were big posters of me all over the room and balloons, candles and streamers were everywhere. I was center stage. My parents and grandparents, pastor and first lady were seated at a table to my right and two tables of aunts, uncles and a few of my cousins were on my left. There was a sea of people all around me. I was trying my best to hold back the tears, but I was losing that battle tremendously. The camera flashes were blinding me and the sweet words of sentiment were so moving. If it weren't so packed, I would have run around the room to hug everyone, but that wasn't going to be possible. At least not like this. I had my McCulley table over there filled with my family from Germany. I couldn't wait to get to that one because we don't get to see each other that often, but when we do we do it up! Oh, look there's my South Carolina Crew. There is STR over there showing out as usual, but I love my boys. I'm looking around but I'm missing something. I lean over and ask Taz where my memory table was and she pointed behind us. Up there on the stage with us was a table dedicated to the loved ones that I had lost over the years. I figured that since they weren't able to be here in person what better way was there to have them be a part of my special day. I had pictures of Mamma, Nana, Daddy D, Uncle Alfred, Pocket, Kerry, Marvin, Uncle Pete, Aunt Mae, Poppa Ron and, of course, Lamont. They each had a candle and a little 'thank you' that I had written in front of them. These people would have been here but God was ready for them in heaven. He left a piece of them in my heart and I wouldn't have it any other way than for them to be behind me supporting me just like they had been doing all the time.

The voice on the microphone caught my attention. It was my mom and she was talking and crying at the same time. Her words brought me to tears and then my daddy talked and then my sister and on and on. The whole time I was just thanking God because this is what life is about. I experienced it all and I made it. God gets all the glory for that.

Then there was a silence in the room that made me wonder who in the world had the microphone. Who could make everyone so quiet and then I heard the voice that motivated me to write this book. Joseph was actually going to say something. He cleared his voice about three times and then J Rock nudged him as if he was a ventriloquist or something and Joseph started to talk. He shared his feelings about the book and told me how proud he was of me and wished me the best and told me he loved me. Those words were paramount because we made it through this disaster together and that meant a lot to me. We were friends more than anything and I loved him, too. We both wanted what was best for each other. He walked over and gave me a hug. I'm sure the stares that he received felt like daggers because I felt a few pierces myself.

The next voice was Will and he was telling me how proud he was of me and how he knew I could do it. He stated that this was going to be the first of many more to come and that he couldn't wait for the next one to come out. He told me he loved me and walked over and kissed me. Okay, if we keep this up, this is going to become 'this is your life' for real and I might not be ready for all of that. My cousins had to be reading my mind because they took over the microphone. They spoke about me being wise beyond my years and how I was the one that kept things going and how they admired my strength and courage. This was heaven on earth and I didn't want this night to end. I got up there with all intentions of being brief and funny, but that didn't happen. It seemed like I thanked everyone that was in the room individually and I was smiling and crying the entire time.

"I realized that there's a purpose for everything that we go through in life. And although we can't explain it and usually don't understand while we're going through it, we should always keep in our minds that God has it for our good." I paused for a moment and then continued.

"Maybe I went through some things so that some of you won't have to. I pray for each of you all the time and I pray that you do the same for me. Now all I have to say is that I love you all and keep the party going!"

And we did just that all night long. I left out of there with my shoes in my hand. We all got in the limos and they took us over to the hotel. You would have thought since we all just spent the past five hours together that we would all just go to sleep. Not! We took that hotel lobby over and the sun was rising when the last of us decided to go to sleep. I strolled to my room with shoes, purse and some of the most beautiful flowers I had ever seen in my hands. I fumbled through my purse looking for my key and finally opened the door. I dropped my shoes at the door and put the other items on the table. I headed for the bathroom and took a nice hot shower to get ready for bed.

I knelt down and said my prayers, climbed into bed and closed my eyes. But just then something popped in my head. Where did I put my journal? I didn't see it anywhere. Then I remembered that there was a note pad on the night stand. I flipped open the cover and began to write faster than I think I had ever written before. As soon as I wrote the last word, I put the pen down and thanked God for his blessings. I read over my work.

The greatest gifts God has given me since His Son Jesus the Christ
Are my mom, dad, family and friends and His favor on my life.
I had a house and money and tons of worldly things
But in the end I lost my peace that only Jesus brings
I lost it all or so it seemed if you measured my worldly possessions
After my anger and many wrong doings finally came my confessions
God opened His arms and called me in and there began my resting
Not my mother or father family or friends could ever provide such blessings
God provided me with everything I needed, and more than I could desire
Simple enough Believing, Loving and Trusting in God is all that was required
Amen!
Divine

Keep Striving!!!